# SAY YOUR PRAYERS

# THOMAS FINCHAM

**Say Your Prayers**
Thomas Fincham

Copyright © 2016
All Rights Reserved.

**AUTHOR'S NOTE**
This book is a work of fiction. Names, characters, places and incidents are products of the author's imagination or are used fictitiously. Any resemblance to actual events or locales or persons, living or dead, is entirely coincidental.

The scanning, uploading and distribution of this book via the internet or any other means without the permission of the publisher is illegal and punishable by law. Please purchase only authorized electronic editions, and do not participate in or encourage electronic piracy of copyrighted materials. Your support of the author's rights is appreciated.

Visit the author's website:
**www.finchambooks.com**

Contact:
**finchambooks@gmail.com**

Join my Facebook page:
**https://www.facebook.com/finchambooks/**

## MARTIN RHODES

1) Close Your Eyes
2) Cross Your Heart
3) Say Your Prayers
4) Fear Your Enemy

# ONE

He strapped his son into the car seat. He made sure the buckles were tight but left enough room for his son to wiggle his body. It was Michael's first day of kindergarten, and Marco could see the eager gleam in his son's eyes.

Each day for the past six months, Michael had gotten up and asked Marco if it was September yet. Marco had made the mistake of telling Michael that in September, he would be old enough to go to school. Hearing this, Michael's first response was, "I'm old enough now, dad." Ever since then, Michael could hardly wait for September. Michael's cousins were already in school. Marco had a feeling this had had a profound effect on his son.

When Marco had told Michael the night before that tomorrow was the big day, he did not expect his son would wake him up bright and early, nor did Marco expect his son to be dressed for the day, but he should have known better. The moment Michael was given the news, he quickly asked his mother to set his clothes out on his bed. He also instructed her to put his lunch in his favorite superhero lunch box.

Marco barely had time to eat breakfast. Michael was already in the hallway wearing his shoes and carrying his backpack.

Marco's wife did not want to go with him to drop off their son. She was already in tears. Her baby was all grown up and ready for school.

The school was only a few blocks away. Marco could have walked his son there, but he wanted to head straight to work after dropping Michael off.

He pulled his minivan up to the front of the school, and the moment he unstrapped his son, the boy grabbed his bag and bolted for the entrance. Michael did not cry, nor did he hug his father. He was too excited to finally be amongst kids his age.

Marco had already met Michael's teacher during orientation. He watched as Michael ran up to her. She held his hand, smiled, and waved at Marco. Marco waved back. His son was in good hands now.

He quickly got into the minivan and drove away. When he was a good distance from the school, tears started flowing down his cheeks. He was not crying because his son was all grown up. He was crying because he wished his own father was alive.

Giuseppe "Joe" Russo was his hero. He died when Marco was not even twelve. Since then, he had wanted a son of his own. He wanted to do everything with his son that he was not able to do with his father.

Marco pulled into the parking lot of a strip mall. He drove around to the back and stopped in front of a sign that read *Joe's Hardware*. The store was once owned and run by Marco's father. His father had worked long hours getting his business up and running, but he loved what he did for a living. Marco and his older brother, Mario, helped out whenever they could. Mario did most of the work while Marco stayed in the back and watched TV.

One day, a customer came into the store and got into an argument with Joe. Marco's father was good with his customers. He was always willing to extend them a line of credit if they needed it. The customer had fallen behind on his payments, and he owed Joe a lot of money. By then, Joe had had enough, and he refused to extend the customer any more credit. The customer, who had been counting on Joe to give him building materials for a project, slapped Joe's desk and started yelling.

Marco was watching cartoons in the back. He heard the commotion and went to see what was going on. He watched as his father demanded that the customer leave the store. When the customer refused, his father physically removed him. His father was a big man, and Marco always felt safe around him.

Marco would never forget what happened next.

The customer came back into the store, carrying a gun. He cursed at his father and fired two shots.

The first hit his father in the stomach, the second in his chest.

Joe Russo died on the floor of his beloved store. His killer was first given a life sentence, but after an appeal, his sentence was reduced to less than ten years. At the time of the incident, the man had been under a lot of stress. His construction business was floundering, and he was on heavy-duty anti-depressants. In addition, the appeals judge disregarded all evidence of the man's behavior with other vendors. He was prone to violent outbursts with them, but the judge considered this not relevant to the case. To make matters worse, the judge and the man's father were once schoolmates in high school, a fact that was only discovered many years later.

Marco was too young to understand anything that was going on, but his mother had made him realize an injustice had been done.

His father's killer was eventually released from prison after serving only half of his sentence. The last Marco had heard, he was operating another construction business with his two sons.

Marco never had the opportunity to do that with his own father.

Soon after his father's death, his mother sold the business to a relative. The relative ran the business for a couple of years until he sold it to a corporation.

As Marco got older, he always wondered what could have been if his father had still been alive. For one thing, he was certain the store would not be called the Building & Supply Store. But when he drove by one day, he saw that the store was for sale. With some money from his older brother and a bank loan, he quickly bought the place. The first thing he did was reinstate the name *Joe's Hardware*. Marco did not know much about running a business, but after a few missteps, the business was now flourishing. He had even rented the stores next to his and expanded his own. He was now one of the largest suppliers of construction materials in Bridgeton. He had over fifteen employees, and he hoped to double that number in a few years.

He parked the minivan. It was early. The store did not open for another hour. He liked coming in when everything was quiet. It allowed him to check the inventory without any interruptions. It also allowed him to soak in and appreciate all that he had accomplished.

Marco knew if his father was alive, he would be proud of him.

He grabbed his lunch and his thermos filled with coffee and got out. He pulled out his keys. When he reached the back door, he stopped.

The door was unlocked.

*What the hell?* he thought. He remembered locking up when he left last night.

He went inside and found the alarm was disabled.

Only Marco and one of his employees knew the alarm code. If Marco was unable to lock up the store, the employee would come and do so, but it was only Marco who opened the store in the morning.

A feeling of dread came over him.

*Did I get robbed?* he thought.

He quickly rushed to the other side of the store where the loading docks were. To his relief, the metal gate was secure. The heavy U-locks remained firmly in place from the inside.

Marco did a quick survey of inventory but could not see anything missing or out of place. He then checked the cash registers and found spare change still in the tills.

He scratched his head. Maybe he had forgotten to lock the back door the night before. This would explain why he did not set the alarm.

He laughed. Everything was fine. There was nothing to be worried about.

He headed in the direction of his office.

That was when he noticed something.

There were only a few drops, but he knew what it was.

*Blood.*

He saw there was a trail leading to the other side of the store. He followed it all the way to the lumber yard.

The drops of blood ended in the middle of the yard. He looked around. He was confused.

He looked up and his mouth dropped.

Hanging from the rafters was a man's body. The body was covered in blood, but it did not take long for Marco to recognize him. He was the man who had shot and killed his father. Marco pulled out his cell phone and quickly dialed 9-1-1.

## TWO

The man lay in the hospital bed with his eyes closed. Tubes ran through his body, and wires attached to his still form projected his vitals on the monitors next to the bed. The man had been in a coma for over three months now. Even in his current state, his wrists were cuffed to the sides of the bed.

Special Agent Johanna "Jo" Pullinger stood before him. She was five-ten and had blonde hair and striking green eyes. Jo was a member of the Federal Bureau of Investigation, and she was there when the man was shot. He had dropped several feet into a tank filled with water and sludge. Jo firmly believed that had the tank been empty, he surely would have died.

His real name was Mathias Lotta, but Jo had known him as Pierre Picaud.

He had seduced her, and she had fallen for him. She had even taken him to meet the people closest to her: her brother and her sister-in-law. On top of that, she had shared her secret with him.

Jo touched her chest. In the last couple of weeks, the pain had resurfaced. She had a heart condition that required a heart transplant. To make matters worse, she had a rare blood type, which meant the prospects of getting the right donor were even slimmer.

Pierre—Mathias—had used her. She was the lead investigator on the Motel Murders case, in which married men were lured into a honey trap by a femme fatale. They were then tortured and shot in the head.

Mathias was the one who had killed them.

During their relationship, she had no idea who he was or what he was capable of.

After his betrayal, her weak heart was left in pieces. She was not sure if it would ever be repaired.

She watched as Mathias lay motionless in bed.

*Is he dreaming?* she thought. *Can he hear me? Does he know he's in custody?*

When the news broke that the FBI was keeping Mathias Lotta alive, there was a public outcry. Everyone wanted them to pull the plug. "Let him die," many people had said.

There was even an attempt on Mathias's life. A masked intruder had somehow gotten into his room and had placed a pillow over his head, but a nurse had walked in and started screaming when she saw what was happening.

The intruder had quickly fled.

Additional security was now stationed outside Mathias's room twenty-four seven.

The families of Mathias's victims were the most vocal pro-death-sentence group. They had staged a rally outside the hospital, demanding justice, and the only justice that was acceptable to them was the death of the man responsible for killing their loved ones. Even the Bridgeton Police Department was in favor of Mathias dying. They had also lost one of their own at his hands.

Detective Jay Crowder had been loaned to the FBI to track down the Motel Murderer. He had worked side-by-side with Jo. But Crowder had made a fatal mistake when he insulted the killer.

His body was discovered at a motel. Jo was too late to save him, but she had almost caught his killer. She did not know at the time that it was Mathias, but now she thought she might understand why he had spared her life when he had a gun aimed at her head.

*Did he have feelings for me?* she wondered. If he did, it would explain why she was still alive. But Jo was confused. A part of her wanted Mathias dead for what he had done to his victims, but another part of her wanted him to recover so that he could be put on trial for the crimes he had committed.

There was another reason she wanted him to live, though. This one was personal. She needed answers. Something bothered her about what happened the night Mathias was shot at the Ashbridges Water Facility.

Mathias had forced Jo to bring his father to the facility. His father had institutionalized his son at a very young age. He had paid an orderly, a nurse, and a psychiatrist to torment him.

Mathias used Craig Orton, the man responsible for the Train Killings, to enact his revenge. He cut off Silvio Tarconi's hands. He cut out Natasha Wedham's eyes. He ripped out Doug Curran's tongue. After Orton's demise, Mathias had killed BN-24 reporter Ellen Sheehan. He had contacted Sheehan to announce when the next Train Killings victim would be found on the subway. His motive was apparently to tie up loose ends. There had been no witnesses to Sheehan's murder, but ballistics had matched Mathias's gun with the bullet that had killed her.

Jo now believed the Motel Murders were a message from Mathias to his father. Mathias blamed his father for the death of his mother, even though it was known that his mother was a victim of the Bridgeton Ripper, a killer responsible for multiple deaths over twenty years before.

What Jo did not understand was why Mathias did not just walk up to his father and shoot him. He despised the man so much that he had set up all these elaborate killings for him, but then he did not shoot his father when he had the chance?

There was more to this than what Jo could see, and the only person who could shed any light on the matter was Mathias Lotta.

Jo's cell phone rang.

# THREE

He was in the parking lot of a fast-food restaurant. He had a cheeseburger in one hand and a large soft drink in the other. A box of onion rings was on the passenger seat. The interior of his Chevy Malibu smelled of fried food.

Martin Rhodes was not overly concerned about the smell. It was not like he was going on a hot date any time soon. In fact, the last person he took out for a movie or dinner was his ex-wife, and that was many years ago.

Rhodes was six-four, and he had salt-and-pepper hair and deep blue eyes.

He took a sip of his drink and then took a big bite out of his sandwich.

Rhodes had spent ten years in prison for murder, a crime he had been clearly guilty of. From the time he had taken aim and pulled the trigger, that moment still haunted him.

With a criminal record, gaining meaningful employment was far more difficult than he had ever imagined. He did not blame potential employers, though. He, too, would be wary of someone who had taken another person's life.

When he was a police detective, Rhodes had always looked at suspects with murder on their records with some suspicion. He always wondered, *If they could kill once, what was to stop them from killing again?* It was like crossing a line with no way back.

If he thought this of others, how could he not expect others to think this of him? In fact, there were times *he* wondered if he could kill again. This deeply troubled him.

Rhodes knew murderers could never be absolved of their crimes, no matter how many years they spent locked up. So, he understood when employers did not return his calls.

Rhodes was, however, more concerned for those with minor offenses. He had met too many in his time behind bars. Many came from rough neighborhoods and broken families. They were picked up for carrying or selling marijuana. Some had been incorrectly charged, and because they did not have the money for bail, they were sent to prison. More often than not, those people pleaded guilty to the offense just to get free. What they did not realize was that they would be left with a criminal conviction on their record. Potential employers did not care how or why you received the conviction. The simple fact that you had one was enough of a red flag.

Rhodes ate the last bite of his sandwich and washed it down with a big sip from his soft drink. At the moment, he was not overly pressed with finding work. He had been lucky. Ever since his release, he had somehow been able to find something to do. First, there was the case in Franklin that involved a man who strangled his victims to death, then there was a case in Parish where his ex-wife wanted him to help exonerate her current husband, and after he came to Bridgeton, he had been hired to investigate two cases. The first was to find the man who had shot and killed a teenager. The second was to find a man who had been legally dead for years.

The last job had paid him handsomely, but Rhodes still did not have a bank account. He did not trust his money to an institution that was charging its clients exorbitant fees for letting them hold their money, which they would, in turn, lend out to others and make more money. Instead, Rhodes kept his cash wrapped in plastic inside his freezer.

Maybe years spent talking to other inmates had made him wary of the powers that be. He used to be on the side of the law, and in many cases, he still was, but he just was not as rigid as he once was about enforcing it.

He realized that the system had failed many people. In fact, it was rigged in favor of those with influence. It was why the prisons were filled with men and women who had been through tough childhoods. When they were old enough, instead of finding a world that would embrace them and give them an opportunity to change their lives, they found a world that shut them out. They had no choice but to continue the life they were raised in.

Rhodes's upbringing was no different, though. He was a petty criminal in his youth, and that was all due to his father, a man who could never hold an honest job. Rhodes, however, was able to turn his life around. Maybe he was one of the fortunate ones.

And the mistake he made, the one that changed his life forever, was not due to any circumstance or his influences from his past; it was done by choice. *He* killed that man, and he paid the price for it, even though his victim had been a child killer. A killer Rhodes had known the law could not touch, and in a fit of anger, he had decided to take matters into his own hands. Rhodes was penitent about his crime, and he scolded others who thought he was a hero.

Rhodes grabbed the onion rings from the passenger seat. They were cold, but he did not care. He washed them down with the remainder of his soda.

Ever since he came into some money, he had been eating out more often. He knew it was not good for his finances or his health, but Rhodes was never good in the kitchen. The moment he got married, it was his wife who had taken care of the cooking. And when he was shipped off to prison, he was given a meal three times a day. Most of the food was bland or inedible, but when he was stuck in a six-by-eight cell for twenty-three of twenty-four hours a day, he looked forward to his breakfast, lunch, and dinner. In fact, he would imagine his meal as if it had come straight from a five-star restaurant. The rubbery meat would turn into a filet mignon covered in gravy. The dry vegetables would turn into a steamy, hot side dish. The cold mashed potatoes would turn into something that had been blended with garlic, butter, and milk. And the expired cranberry juice would turn into chilled, fine wine. Coping with prison fare was all in how he approached it, just like he approached the rest of his time in prison.

He took a similar approach to life now that he was a free man. This was why he made sure to keep his expenses low. He lived in the basement of an apartment house. He could move and get a nicer place, but for now, his current residence was serving its purpose. He did not own a cell phone. He used a pay phone down the block from his apartment instead. He did not smoke, but he occasionally drank beer.

He frequented diners and bars only because it allowed him to get out of his apartment. Plus, he needed a place to think.

As a detective, he used to always be out and about, which meant he ate wherever he could. It was the one habit he did not mind continuing.

He stuffed the sandwich wrapper, soft drink cup, and empty onion ring box in the paper bag, and he threw it in a garbage can as he drove out of the parking lot.

# FOUR

Jo pulled her Jetta into the parking lot of the strip mall. There were already police cruisers and Bureau-issued vehicles in front of the hardware store.

Jo got out of her car, walked up to the yellow police tape, and flashed her credentials to the officer protecting the crime scene.

She entered the premises and immediately spotted her supervisor.

Special Agent in Charge Charlotte Walters was standing next to the cashier station. Her face was etched with deep wrinkles from years of heavy smoking. She had quit a long time ago, but the effects of her habit were still visible on her face. One could mistake her gray eyes as being devoid of life, but in fact, her eyes always had a calculating look to them, as if Walters was trying to keep up with all the cases her office was currently working on.

Jo had gotten used to seeing her boss with another person whenever she approached a new crime scene. Walters was usually arguing with Chief Vincent Baker of the Bridgeton Police Department. Baker would normally be stressing to her that the crime scene was under the BPD's jurisdiction. Walters, on the other hand, would be explaining why the FBI should be in charge of the investigation.

After Detective Crowder's death, however, Baker had backed off. He had, in fact, become more guarded with his force. It was Baker who had insisted that Crowder be put on the Motel Murders case, so he felt responsible for what ended up happening to him.

In a twisted way, Walters also felt responsible for what happened to Crowder. During the Motel Murders investigation, Crowder had reported to her. But he had stepped out of line by getting drunk and disorderly while off duty, and Walters had no choice but to request his removal from the case. She believed if Crowder was still on duty, he would not have been alone when the killer lured him to his death. Jo disagreed with her. Walters or even Baker were not guilty of Crowder's death. It was Mathias Lotta who had brutally murdered him in cold blood. There was no way for them to know Crowder would end up being a target. On top of that, they couldn't possibly keep a watchful eye on those who reported to them at all times. It was only a matter of time before Mathias had found a way to get to Crowder. Jo did, however, regret not seeing through Mathias's lies sooner. Had she done that, or had her team gotten a solid lead, maybe Crowder would still be alive.

Jo walked up to Walters and asked, "What do we have today?" The only information Jo had was that a dead body had been found at a hardware store.

Walters replied, "Victim is fifty-nine, Caucasian, runs a construction company, and his name is George Moll."

"How do you know the victim's name?" Jo asked, curious.

Walters nodded in the direction of another man. He was sitting in a chair near the aisles. An officer was standing next to him.

"Who is he?" Jo asked.

"His name is Marco Russo, and he's the owner of the hardware store. He told us the victim's name."

Jo looked at Walters. "They knew each other?"

"You won't believe what I'm about to tell you next," Walters said. "Many years ago, the victim shot and killed Russo's father."

Jo raised an eyebrow. "Really?"

"And here's the kicker. He killed him in this very store."

Jo looked in Russo's direction. "He told you?"

"Yes."

"And you believe him?"

"Why would he lie?" Walters replied. "Plus, I'm familiar with the case."

"Do you think he did it for revenge?" Jo asked, keeping her eyes on Russo.

"If he did, he'd be stupid to leave the body in his own store."

Jo was thinking the same thing. "And he called it in?"

Walters nodded. "He said he came in this morning and found the back door unlocked. He thought he'd been robbed, but when he searched the store, he discovered the body."

"Where is it?"

"I'll show you."

Jo followed Walters to the other side of the store. She entered what looked like the lumber yard. Walters pointed at the ceiling. Jo looked up and saw the body hanging from the rafters.

"Someone went through a lot of trouble to display that for us," Jo said.

"Or for him," Walters said.

"You mean Russo?"

"Who else?" Walters replied. "The victim killed Russo's father, and someone killed him and left him as a souvenir for Russo."

"And we are sure Russo didn't do it?" Jo asked.

"We are never sure of anything until the case is closed. But I keep asking myself, why leave evidence in a place he owns and operates that could incriminate him? Also, why kill the victim now after so many years?"

"Maybe Russo suddenly snapped," Jo suggested.

Walters shook her head. "I doubt that."

Jo's eyes narrowed. "Why are you so sure of Russo's innocence? It's usually *you* who is telling me I should consider everyone a suspect."

Walters looked away. "It's because I handled Russo's father's case all those years ago. Russo doesn't remember me. He was too young. But I got to know his mother. They were a close-knit family, and the death of Joe Russo was a devastating blow to them. I was grateful to know that Joe's son had taken over the family business. Russo has a young son of his own. I doubt he'd do anything that would jeopardize the well-being of his family."

Jo did not know what to say.

# FIVE

A man walked up to Jo and Walters. Ben Nakamura was the Bureau's Medical Examiner. Ben was short, chubby, and known for wearing colorful t-shirts and matching watches. That day, he was wearing a bright green t-shirt, a green watch, green glasses, and even green sneakers. He looked like an overweight turtle.

"Let me guess," Jo said. "You're wearing green socks."

Ben smiled. "And green underwear."

Jo made a face. "I really didn't need to know that."

Walters shook her head. "I'll leave you two. Let me know what you find." She walked away.

Ben said to Jo, "Has he woken up?"

Jo knew he was referring to Mathias. When Jo had known him as Pierre Picaud, she had told Ben all about him. Ben was suspicious. He asked her a lot of questions about Mathias, and Jo did not have all the answers. She knew at the time that Ben was being protective of her. He did not want to see her get hurt. Ben was also one of her confidants. Whatever she told him would stay with him, which was why he was one of the few people who knew of her heart condition.

Ben had insisted from day one that she get the transplant, but she had brushed the topic aside.

Ben also knew of her obsession with finding the Bridgeton Ripper. Special Agent William "Bill" Pullinger was Jo's father, and he was one of the Ripper's victims. Even to this day, Jo was deeply bothered because she could not find the person responsible for his death.

Jo shook her head. "I came straight from the hospital. His condition has not changed."

Ben grimaced.

"If you're going to say 'I told you so,'" Jo said, "please don't."

"I was actually going to say I'm sorry," Ben said. "I really hoped things would work out between you two."

She nodded.

Ben's face suddenly brightened up. "You wanna examine the victim?" he asked, rubbing his hands with glee.

"Yes."

Ben looked up at the rafters. "Then, it might be best if we bring him down."

It took two Bridgeton police officers to climb a long ladder and slowly and carefully pull the body down. It was believed the killer had tied a rope around the victim's chest, tugging the rope underneath his armpits. The killer had then swung the rope around a rafter and, after creating a pulley, the killer pulled the victim up towards the ceiling.

Once the body was on the ground, it did not take long for Jo and Ben to see that his throat had been slit from ear to ear. *That would explain the amount of dried blood on him*, Jo thought.

Ben knelt down and quickly inspected the body.

Jo asked, "Is there any message on him?"

"You mean like the other murders?" Ben was referring to the Train Killings and the Motel Murders.

Ben quickly checked the victim's chest, back, and torso. He shook his head.

Jo was not sure why she was interested in finding out. Mathias was directly or indirectly involved in the train and motel deaths, which involved messages left at the crime scenes, but he was now in a coma, so there was no possible way for him to be linked to Moll's death.

"Wait," Ben said. "Look."

On the right palm of the victim, the word *Justice* was written with a permanent marker, and on the left palm, the word *Served* was written.

"*Justice served?*" Jo said, surprised.

Ben said, "I heard you and Walters talking. Maybe this does have something to do with what happened to Russo's father many years ago."

Jo hoped he was wrong. The last thing she wanted was a vigilante killer roaming the streets of Bridgeton, dispensing his or her own form of justice.

# SIX

Jo was in Russo's cramped office. Russo was sitting behind the computer with a monitor and keyboard before him.

There were several cameras inside and outside the store. Security was a top priority for Russo. *That is a good thing*, Jo thought. There was a chance they could see the perpetrator.

They watched the six separate camera views visible on the monitor. The first two were focused on the front and back doors of the store. The third was focused directly on the loading dock. The fourth was aimed at the cashiers' station. The last two were overviews of the various store aisles.

Jo was most interested in the first two.

They watched as the clock ticked below the screens.

"Can you fast-forward it?" Jo asked.

Russo did as instructed.

At around two o'clock in the morning, a white cargo van pulled up to the back of the store. The van stopped, and for several minutes, nothing happened.

"Can you see the license plate?" Jo asked.

Russo shook his head. "Not from this angle. Let me rewind the footage." He did. The van pulled up to the store again. Russo slowed the footage, and that's when they realized the license plate had been removed.

"Damn," Jo said. "Let it play."

The van's driver-side door opened. A figure dressed in black emerged. Jo could quickly tell it was a man from the shape of the body. His dark outfit was topped off with a balaclava and gloves.

Jo gritted her teeth. There was no way for them to see who the man was.

The man went around to the back of the van and, a few seconds later, pulled out George Moll's body. He grabbed the victim's arms and dragged him to the back door. The man removed a key, unlocked the door, and then punched in a code on the security panel.

Russo jumped from his chair. "How did he know the password?" he exclaimed.

Jo was not sure, but she did not like what she was seeing.

They focused their attention on the next camera. They watched as the man dragged the victim to an area inside the store. He lay the body down and then looked around.

Jo squinted. The drops of blood she had seen on the floor must have gotten there when the perpetrator had paused to catch his breath.

The man then continued moving the body. They knew where he was taking it.

The camera flipped to the lumber yard. The perpetrator dragged the body to the middle of the open space.

He then disappeared from view.

"Where did he go?" Jo asked.

Russo checked all the camera angles and finally found the man again. He was carrying a bundle of rope.

*He must have picked it up from one of the aisles*, Jo thought.

The man created a loop and placed it around the victim's chest.

What happened next, Jo could not have predicted. Instead of hurling the rope around the rafters and then pulling the victim up, the man disappeared from view again. He returned, driving a four-wheel stock picker.

Russo said, "We use it to stock heavy items on the higher shelves."

The man placed the body on the machine. He then got on as well and proceeded to raise himself and the body up.

When he was high enough, he swung the rope around the rafters, tied it, and then lowered the machine.

Slowly, the rope pulled the body in the air.

Once he was on the ground, the man parked the stock picker in a corner. Then he left the store, got in the van, and drove off.

Jo was bothered by how casual the perpetrator had acted. She also wondered how he had disabled security so easily. "Who else knows your alarm codes?" Jo asked Russo.

"Me and my store manager, Miguel Pinetta," Russo replied.

"Where is he?"

"He should be here by now."

Russo left the office. He returned a couple of minutes later, looking grim. "Miguel didn't come in today."

"Does he usually call to let you know if he's not coming?"

"All the employees have to. That's our policy."

"Did you call him?" Jo asked.

"I just did right now. He's not picking up."

"Can you give me his address?"

Ben ran up to Jo as she was leaving the store. "I did a quick examination of the body, and I think I've found something that might interest you," he said.

"What?" Jo asked.

"The victim's neck was slit open with a sharp blade."

"I think I could tell that just by looking at the body."

"But the cut is so precise that it severed the main arteries. I have a strong feeling it was done in order to drain his blood."

Jo's eyes widened.

"Something feels familiar about this case," Ben said, staring at the floor.

"What?"

"I don't know. But I see red flags."

"Well, let me know when something pops out."

Jo quickly left.

# SEVEN

Rhodes pulled up to his apartment house and found Tess waiting for him.

Tess Connelly was his neighbor. She and her mom lived on the top floor. His landlady lived on the main level, and Rhodes lived in the basement. Normally, Tess would be dressed in baggy clothes. That day, however, she wore a blouse, fitted pants, and heeled boots. She did have on her usual dark mascara and dark lipstick, and her hair was shaped in the tomboy haircut she usually sported.

Rhodes was about to comment on her change of attire but then held his tongue. *It is a nice look on her*, he thought. *If she grew her hair a bit more, she would go from pretty to beautiful.*

There was another reason Rhodes still had not moved from the small basement apartment. He felt protective of Tess. It was almost fatherly, even though Rhodes had no desire to have any children of his own.

"What're you doing outside?" Rhodes asked.

Rhodes had given Tess a key in case of an emergency. If she had family problems—most likely a spat with her mother—he did not want her sitting on his front steps.

The weather had gotten a bit cooler, and he still refused to let her use his car as a place of refuge. The last time he did, it nearly got her killed when she became a hostage of Craig Orton, the Train Killer.

"There's a man inside your apartment," she said.

"Sully?"

Tess shook her head. "It's not your father."

Rhodes frowned. "How did he get in my apartment?"

"I let him in."

"Why would you let him in?" he asked.

"He said he was your friend," she replied.

Rhodes did not have any friends, unless he counted Detective Tom Nolan. He was the only friend who knew Rhodes's current address.

"Did he give you a name?"

She shook her head. "I didn't ask."

"And you believed him when he said he was my friend?"

She shrugged. "He showed me his badge. I think he's a cop or a detective."

Rhodes's eyes narrowed. *It has to be Nolan*, he thought. But he knew Nolan would not show up unannounced. Plus, Franklin was a good couple of hours away. He would have at least told him he was coming down.

"Everything okay?" Tess asked. "Did I do something wrong?"

"No, everything is fine," Rhodes replied. "Next time anyone shows up, tell them to wait outside."

Rhodes moved to his front door. He wished he had a weapon on him, but as a convicted felon, he was not legally allowed to carry one. It was not like he would pull a gun on a police officer if in fact the person inside was a cop. But having a weapon would have made him feel a little more secure.

He opened the door and went in.

Sitting at his small dining table was a man. His face was hard, and his nose was twisted and flat as if it had taken too many punches. His head was shaved, and he had on a cheap three-piece suit.

Rhodes immediately recognized him. Leonard "Mac" MacAfferty used to be a detective for the Newport Police Department when Rhodes was a detective there as well. Mac and Rhodes were not only colleagues but also good friends. Unfortunately, their friendship had ended bitterly.

While Rhodes had an obsessive personality, Mac had an addictive one, but he always managed to do his job without it affecting him. However, Mac's penchant for addiction became a problem when he was called in to investigate the death of a man during an underground poker tournament held in someone's basement. The man had died from a heart attack, and Mac's investigation was quickly closed. But Mac was intrigued by the amount of money the players were making in these illegal tournaments. Against his better judgment, he began frequenting all the poker joints in Newport. He would spend entire nights playing against people who were far more skilled at the game than he was. He would lose hundreds, even thousands, of dollars on one hand. It got so bad that Mac soon found himself broke. To make matters worse, Mac started cutting corners in his detective duties. His work became sloppy, and in some cases, the judge threw out his evidence because it was improperly obtained.

His career as a cop came to an end when he took a job from a known loan shark in order to repay him for the debt he owed. The loan shark had a delinquent client. Mac used his badge to enter the client's house and used his government-issued weapon to threaten him. The man paid up, but not before Mac broke his jaw.

Mac realized he had gone too far. He broke down and confessed to Rhodes. Rhodes, in turn, told his superiors.

Mac was swiftly suspended without pay, and he blamed Rhodes for his apparent betrayal. Rhodes did not see it like that. He had witnessed Mac spiral downward, and he had, on numerous occasions, not only backed him up but also tried to help him. The incident involving the loan shark client was simply the last straw.

Rhodes knew Mac cared deeply about being a detective and hoped the threat of Mac losing his badge would be the catalyst that would finally force him back on the right path.

Instead, Mac went in the opposite direction. He quit his job and began working for the loan shark. He became an enforcer, and he was very good at it. There were many incidents of people showing up in the ER with broken jaws, ribs, and noses. Rumor had it that Mac was responsible for the injuries.

Mac never forgave Rhodes for what he had done, and Rhodes never forgave Mac for the way he ended up. He never imagined his friend would stoop so low as to become a bully and a thug. Rhodes always considered Mac a criminal. It was only after he became a criminal himself that he realized he could have handled the situation a little differently. Mac needed help, but instead of helping him, Rhodes had pushed him away.

"How're you doing, Martin?" Mac asked. He had a bottle in front of him. "I hope you don't mind that I grabbed a beer from your fridge. I got thirsty waiting for you."

Rhodes did not move. He stood by the door

"You look good," Mac said. "Not as heavy as I last remembered you."

Rhodes used to be overweight. Working long hours solving cases had relegated his regimen to junk food and no exercise. He was back to eating fast food again, but at least he was working out each morning, something he had picked up while he was in prison.

"How did you find me?" Rhodes asked. "It's not like I'm listed in the phone directory."

"I spoke to your buddy, Tom Nolan."

"And he gave you my address?"

"Not exactly," Mac replied. "Apparently, he is close to a reporter in Franklin. They share quite a lot with each other."

Rhodes understood. "You're talking about Hyder Ali. And he told you."

"Well, I wouldn't say he came forward on his own. I had to use a little persuasion."

Rhodes crossed his arms over his chest. Mac quickly put his hands up. "No, I didn't coerce or threaten him, if that's what you think. I told him I was a friend of yours and it was urgent that I talk to you. It helps when you have old photos of us together."

"So, you used our past history to get the information you needed," Rhodes said.

Mac smiled. "It's a trick we learned as detectives, didn't we?"

"What're you doing here, Mac?"

"I thought I'd grab a drink with my friend, like the old times, you know."

Rhodes still did not move. He was not buying it. Mac had vowed to destroy him for what he had done to him. If Rhodes was in his place right now, he would have already taken a swipe at him.

*So, what is all this about?* Rhodes thought.

Mac read his face. He put his hand in his suit jacket.

Rhodes straightened up.

"Relax," Mac quickly said. "I'm not here to shoot you." He pulled out his hand. In it was a law enforcement badge.

Rhodes said, "My neighbor told me you had shown it to her. I didn't know you were desperate enough to carry a fake badge."

"It's not fake, Martin. I'm back at Newport Police Department."

Rhodes stared at the badge. He had recurring dreams that *he* was back with Newport PD as a detective and that he had never spent any time in prison. But those dreams were more like nightmares because they reminded him that he would never be a detective again.

"Martin," Mac said. "I'm here because I need your help."

# EIGHT

Jo knocked on the door and waited. The apartment building was located in an industrial part of the city. During her drive over, she had spotted several factories and manufacturing plants. Placed strategically between them were many low-rise buildings. The owners of these buildings understood that employees of the local industries needed a place to live. The buildings were not in great shape, but the people who resided in them did so for the cheap rent and the convenience of living close to their workplace.

Miguel Pinetta lived in one of these buildings. Even though his commute to the hardware store was over an hour, the low rent was something he could not ignore.

Jo knocked on the door again. No one answered.

She pulled out her weapon, steadied herself, and kicked the door in.

The moment the door swung in, she saw what looked like drops of blood in the hallway.

The lights were on, and there was a sound coming from another room. She carefully moved in.

When she reached the living room, she holstered her weapon.

Slumped on the sofa was the body of a man. Jo did not have to examine him to know it was Miguel Pinetta.

Miguel's head was tilted sideways. Jo could see a black hole in his forehead. Dried blood streaked his face and was caked underneath his nostrils.

The TV across from him was still on. On the coffee table before him was a plate of rice, chicken, and a bottle of beer. *Most likely, his dinner from last night*, Jo thought.

She took a deep breath and exhaled.

Jo pieced together what must have happened. Miguel had just sat down to have dinner and watch TV when there was a knock at the door. The moment he opened it, the killer had hit him squarely in the face, perhaps breaking his nose. That would explain the blood in the hallway. The killer must have then aimed the gun at Miguel and told him to sit down on the sofa.

*But why?*

She knew the answer. The killer wanted information. He wanted the password to the security alarm.

Once the killer got what he wanted, he had shot Miguel between the eyes.

Jo moved around the apartment. It was sparingly furnished, as if Miguel was being frugal with his money, or was sending most of his pay elsewhere.

Jo found her latter hunch was right when she found stacks of what looked like money transfer slips lying on the kitchen counter. They were all to an address in the Philippines. On the refrigerator were photos of a woman and two kids. Jo could only guess that they were Miguel's wife and children.

She went out into the hallway and found a jacket hanging on a hook. She put her hand inside the pockets and pulled out a wallet. It did not appear as if anything had been taken from the wallet, but in it, she found an insurance document for a cargo van.

So, it *was* Miguel's vehicle the killer had driven to drop off George Moll's body.

Jo looked around and could not find the keys. This further confirmed her hunch.

She pulled out her cell phone and dialed the FBI's Bridgeton office number.

# NINE

Rhodes reluctantly pulled up a chair across from Mac. He sat down and crossed his arms over his chest. He was not exactly sure what Mac's motives were, but he would at least give him the courtesy of hearing him out.

Mac said, "I want to make something clear right from the beginning. I've gotten treatment for my addictions, and I've worked extremely hard to get back into the position I'm in now."

Rhodes knew he was referring to his position as a detective.

"It wasn't easy," Mac continued, "but there were people at the department who were willing to forgive me for my mistakes."

Rhodes wished it were the same for him, but that was just a pipe dream. No one could forgive murder, even if it was of a person responsible for the brutal death of a toddler. Plus, even if he somehow managed to get back on the Newport PD's payroll, the public would have a fit. They would cause such a fuss that in order to save face, the department would have to fire him.

Rhodes respected the profession too much to have anything negatively affect it. The job had been good to him. It had given him purpose and stability. His childhood had none of that. He was lost then, and he was involved in activities that skirted the law.

His father was a big reason for that. And it was why Rhodes had vowed to show the old man that he was different than him. When he graduated from the police academy, the first thing he did was send a photo of himself dressed in uniform to his father. He wanted his old man to know that the Rhodes men were no longer criminals, a trait which had started with his grandfather and moved on to his father, and now would end with Martin.

However, things did not work out the way he had hoped and planned.

Mac said, "Getting a second chance was a lifesaver for me, and I mean that literally. I was doing stuff I was not proud of. I was in a dark place, a hole so deep I thought I would never get out of it. When I heard that you had gone to prison, I was overjoyed. I'm not going to lie about that. I thought you deserved what you got for what you did to me. But instead of feeling great about my situation, I felt even worse. I realized you were not to blame for what had happened to me. I'd messed up. You were only trying to get me on the right path. I wrote you a couple of times when you were in prison. I wanted to ask for forgiveness, but I guess you were in a darker place than I was, so I wasn't offended when you didn't write back."

Rhodes had received the letters but never opened them. He had never opened any mail he received while he was locked up. He did not want to know what the letters were about because he could not do anything for those who wrote to him. He did not feel the need to contact anyone outside, nor did he feel a need to ask for anyone's help. In his opinion, doing so was pointless.

"Anyway," Mac said, "ever since I've been reinstated, I've been focused on my job. I never realized how much I missed it. I've been lucky to solve a couple of tough cases, but there is one I can't seem to crack."

Rhodes narrowed his eyes. "And you want me to help you?"

"Yes."

Rhodes looked away. "You know I can't perform investigative services. I'm a convicted felon. I can't get a license."

If Mac was trying to bait him, Rhodes had to make sure to let him know he would not take the bait. There were only a handful of people Rhodes trusted, and Mac was not one of them.

Mac smiled. "I know what you're thinking, and no, I'm not here to get you locked up again. I hold no grudge against you, Martin. Why would I? I've got my life back, and you—" He paused as if to carefully choose his next words. "You have a long uphill battle to regain whatever life you previously had."

Rhodes stared at him.

"If it helps, I won't pay you," Mac said. "Even though I know you've already been compensated for such services."

"I was only acting as a consultant," Rhodes said.

"Say what you like, but the Bridgeton newspapers think you had a hand in solving some pretty outrageous cases. What did they call them? The Train Killings and the Motel Murders, I believe."

"It wasn't me. It was the FBI," Rhodes said.

"Regardless, you were deeply involved, I'm sure."

"What's your point?"

"I'm not here to hurt you, Martin. All I need is for you to give me your opinion on a case. I'll give you all I have on the file. I could get in trouble for this. I'm providing information in an ongoing investigation to someone not involved in the case, but it's a risk I'm willing to take for you to trust me."

Rhodes stared at Mac for a minute, then he nodded. "Okay, tell me about it."

# TEN

Mac took a sip of his beer and said, "Six months ago, a father and daughter were found dead in a nice suburban house. The father—Myron Goldsmith, aged fifty-two—was the president of a large technology firm. The daughter—Jenny Goldsmith, aged twenty-one—was a student at Ryerson Interior Design College. Both victims were found with multiple stab wounds." Mac paused. "Let me clarify. Jenny was found with over fifty stab wounds while Mr. Goldsmith was stabbed over a dozen times. Jenny's body was found on the stairs, and Mr. Goldsmith's was found at the entrance of the house. We believe the killer rang the doorbell, and when Mr. Goldsmith opened the door, the killer attacked him. Hearing his screams, Jenny came running down the stairs, and that's when she was attacked. Mrs. Goldsmith and their teenage son were at a soccer game. I believe if they had been home that night, they too would've ended up dead. In fact, Mr. Goldsmith was not supposed to be home that night, either. He was supposed to be out with his friends bowling, but for some reason, he canceled at the last minute. This makes me think that the killer knew the Goldsmiths' schedule and that his target was the daughter."

"*He*?" Rhodes said. "You have a suspect?"

"Adam Channing, aged twenty-nine, no fixed address, used to be in a foster home but has now been sleeping on friends' couches. He dated Jenny briefly, but then they broke up."

"Who broke up with whom?" Rhodes found himself asking questions like a detective.

Mac smiled. "She did, and we think he was upset about being dumped, so he went after her."

Rhodes frowned. "I'm assuming you don't have any proof of this, or why else would you be here?"

Mac nodded. "When we narrowed our focus, Adam became our prime suspect. When we brought him in for questioning, we found a journal on him. It was entirely devoted to Jenny. There were even poems about her."

"He wrote them?"

"Yep. And we found photos of her glued to the pages, names of her friends, what she liked, what she disliked, what classes she was taking, what her teachers' names were, stuff on her family. This guy was obsessed with her."

Rhodes looked down at the table. "That still doesn't point to him being the killer." Rhodes was playing devil's advocate, and he hoped Mac would come back with something more solid.

Mac leaned closer. "I found strands of her hair taped to the pages."

"So why haven't you linked him to the murders?"

"He has an alibi."

"Who's the alibi?"

"The friend he was staying with. On the night of the murders, they were at a rock concert. They have tickets to prove it."

"So what? They could've bought the tickets months ago."

"Right, so I went down to the concert venue. I showed them his photo, and the security guys confirmed seeing him come in with his friend. They also saw him leave. The duration of the concert is around the time Jenny and her father were murdered. The coroner confirmed the timings."

Rhodes pondered Mac's information. "How sure were the security guys? I mean, there must have been thousands of spectators at the concert."

"They were very sure. Apparently, Adam had too much to drink that night, and he became very rowdy. He was hollering and screaming outside the venue. He kept yelling that it was the best show he had ever been to."

"What did security do?"

"They told his friend to take him home, or else they'd call the police. It was at the end of the concert, so there were already some drunken fans."

"Where is Adam now?"

"After talking to him, we had to let him go."

Rhodes thought for a moment. "I don't know how I can help you, Mac. I mean, for every one case we solve, there are probably five or six that end up as cold cases. It's the nature of the job. You know it better than I do."

Mac sighed. "I gave my word to Jenny's mother that I would find her daughter and husband's killer."

Rhodes frowned. He knew detectives made promises like that all the time. They wanted to assure the grieving family members that they would not rest until they had found and punished the person who had destroyed their lives. "It still doesn't explain why you need my help."

"I also gave my word to Megan."

Rhodes had forgotten Mac had a daughter. When Mac's marriage fell apart, it was Megan who had suffered the most. Rhodes felt guilty that perhaps it was his action that may have tipped the marriage over. He knew, of course, that was not correct. Mac's reckless behavior had impacted not only his work but also his personal life.

Mac said, "Jenny was Megan's best friend."

*So, that's what this is all about*, Rhodes thought. *He gave his word to his daughter that he would find her best friend's killer. Why didn't he just say so?*

"Martin," Mac said, "Adam Channing is shady. He had a motive and the means to do it."

"But he also has an alibi."

"Right, but I know he did it. And I need your help to prove it."

Rhodes was not convinced. "I don't know."

"Listen, this guy can and will disappear if I don't charge him with something soon. He has spent his entire life bouncing from one foster home to another. Right now, I've managed to get eyes on him so that he doesn't run, but the captain has given me a deadline before he pulls the plug. There are only so many resources we have at our disposal. I am running out of time, Martin."

Rhodes stood up and looked out the basement window. "I can't go back to Newport. I just can't. It'll open a lot of wounds."

"I understand. That's why I'll be your eyes and ears in Newport. All you have to do is go over the file and let me know if I missed anything."

He placed a thick folder on the table.

Rhodes hesitated.

"Please, Martin. Do it for old times' sake."

Rhodes did owe him for what he did to him. It was one of the things that deeply bothered him when he was stuck in prison. He always wished he could go back and change how he had handled the situation with Mac.

"Okay, I'll have a look at it," he finally said.

# ELEVEN

Jo was in her Jetta when she received the call. She swung the car around and drove in the other direction.

Half an hour later, she was standing before a storefront. There was no sign outside, and the blinds were shut.

She waited a minute before the door swung open. A man with grayish hair, a pot belly, and smelling of cigarettes said, "You are the detective?"

"Special agent." Jo flashed her credentials.

"Slaven Nostorovic," he said, extending his hand. Jo shook it. She noticed his palm was calloused.

"Come in," Nostorovic said.

Jo entered and found herself in an area that reeked of sweat and cigarettes. There were several tables with chairs around them. Playing cards were scattered on the tables. There was a pool table in the corner with a dartboard next to it and a large flat-screen TV just across from the table. There was also a fridge at the other end of the room.

"What is this place?" Jo asked.

Nostorovic smiled as if he was glad she asked the question. "It's sort of like an old men's club. All the guys that come here have worked for years in the construction industry. Some were members of the same union, some worked with the same company, while others worked independently in the business. We've known each other for years. We meet in the evenings, so that's why it's empty right now. It's a place to get away from work, family, or whatever else that's bothering you. Once a month, we collect money to pay for the rent. We bring our own alcohol and cigarettes, so we don't need a license to sell tobacco and liquor. It's all legit."

"I'm sure it is," Jo said. "I'm more interested in what you know about George Moll."

He frowned. "I heard about what happened to him."

Jo wanted to know how he had found out so quickly, but she realized the Bureau must have already provided a statement to the media.

"Do you know who did it?" Nostorovic asked.

Jo shook her head.

"Most of the guys still don't know," he said. "Or else my phone would be ringing off the hook."

"George Moll," Jo said, bringing the focus back to the victim. "What can you tell me about him?"

"I can tell you he was here last night."

"What time?" Jo asked.

"He came around seven, and I think he left after ten."

*That is a couple of hours before the killer brought his body into the hardware store*, Jo thought.

"Did he tell you where he was going when he left?" Jo asked.

"I think he was going home. He'd had a beer or two, so I made sure he wasn't drunk getting behind the wheel. He wasn't, so I let him go. But when I was leaving last night, I found his car parked in the back. I thought maybe he'd realized he was a bit wobbly and decided to take a taxi. When I came in this morning, his car was still here."

"Show me," Jo said.

They walked out to the back parking lot. A Ford pickup truck was parked next to a Mitsubishi.

"The truck belongs to George," he said.

Jo walked around the car. It was still locked.

"Do you have security cameras?" Jo asked.

He shook his head. "Why would we need them? We have nothing valuable for anyone to steal."

Jo did not think they would, but it was worth a shot. *The killer must have scoped out the location beforehand and chosen this place to grab Moll*, she thought.

Jo pulled out her cell phone. "We're going to take the truck in for further inspection."

"Sure," Nostorovic said.

Suddenly, his cell phone buzzed. He checked it. "I think the guys just heard the news."

# TWELVE

Jo checked her watch and decided to take a detour. She was supposed to head back to the office, but instead, she felt like she wanted to be someplace else.

She drove around until she found parking. She got out and immediately knew she had made the right decision.

The air was cool and crisp. The sun was strong and bright.

In the distance, she saw a woman pushing a girl on a swing. There were other children on the playground, but Jo focused only on her.

The girl laughed as the woman pushed her higher and higher. Across from them, a woman was throwing a Frisbee for her dog to catch. Not far from her, three boys were kicking a soccer ball. Over on the other side of the park, a man and a woman were lying on the grass, soaking in the sun.

*Why don't I get out more often and enjoy the beauty around me?* Jo wondered. Ever since Mathias went into a coma, all she had obsessed about was finding out what he wanted to tell her. There was a reason he had brought them to the water facility, and Jo had a feeling he wanted them to know something. Instead, his father shot him, and now Mathias was hooked up to wires and tubes. There was no telling how long he would stay like that. Three months had already passed. Jo had once read that a man had been in a coma for over thirty years before he finally woke up. She could not wait that long. There was a strong possibility she might not be alive with her heart condition.

Suddenly, a girl squealed. Jo looked up and smiled.

A girl was running toward her with her arms open.

Jo grabbed her and hugged her tight.

Chrissy was four years old, and she was Jo's niece.

"Aunty Jo," Chrissy said. "Where have you been?"

"I've been busy, sweetheart."

"I missed you."

"I missed you too," Jo said, feeling guilty. She had been so preoccupied with her own problems that she had not visited Chrissy in weeks. It was not like Jo did not think about her. There were times she had driven to her home, but if the lights were not on, she would just drive away. She would tell herself that she would come back when she had more time.

A woman approached them. She had straight, dark hair. Her skin was black, and when the sun hit her face, it almost looked like she sparkled. She had one of the most beautiful smiles Jo had ever seen.

Kim Davis-Pullinger was Jo's sister-in-law. She also happened to be closer to Jo than her brother, Sam.

"You haven't dropped by for dinner," Kim said.

Jo used to regularly go to her brother's house at the end of each day. There were several reasons for that: One, she could not really cook. Two, she did not have time to learn. Three, she wanted to spend as much time with her only niece as possible.

"I'm sorry," Jo said. "I've had a lot on my plate."

"Sam told me what happened." Jo knew she was referring to Mathias. When he was masquerading as Pierre, Jo had taken him to Chrissy's birthday party. Jo had to dress up like a princess, and Mathias wore a suit that made him look like a prince. She remembered thinking at the time that she was the luckiest person in the world and that her dreams had finally come true. Within a few days, those dreams had quickly turned into a nightmare.

"How is Sam?" Jo asked.

Samuel "Sam" Pullinger was two years older than Jo. He worked for the government as a forensic accountant. His job involved monitoring and investigating financial crimes. With the state of the current economy, Sam was busier than ever. He was working seven days a week. He was sometimes away for days, leaving Kim to take on more parental duties.

Jo knew all this because Kim had told her. Sam was not good at keeping in touch, but Kim was. It was another reason Jo got along with Kim. The two women had one person in common: Sam.

"Sam is good," Kim said, but then she looked away.

Jo turned to Chrissy. "Why don't you go on the slides so that I can talk to mommy?"

"You promise you'll come and push me on the swings?" Chrissy asked.

"I promise."

"Pinky promise?" Chrissy stuck out her little finger.

"Pinky promise," Jo said, entwining her little finger with Chrissy's.

When Chrissy was too far away to hear them, Jo asked Kim, "Is everything okay?"

Kim hesitated.

"You can talk to me," Jo said. "We're family."

"It's your brother," Kim said.

Jo felt a pang of worry. "What about him?"

"We're going through a rough patch. He's hardly ever home. Even when he is, his mind is elsewhere."

"It must be his work."

"I don't know. He won't talk to me. I don't remember the last time we had dinner together as a family."

"Is it because I haven't shown up?" Jo asked.

"Of course not," Kim replied. "We know how busy you are when you're involved in an investigation. It just feels different between Sam and me now. We used to always spend evenings and weekends doing things as a family. But now it just feels like Sam is somehow more detached. It's so bad that I've contemplated leaving him."

Jo felt a stabbing pain in her chest. She controlled herself so that Kim did not see. She did not want to scare her.

"Do you want me to talk to him?" Jo asked.

Kim shook her head. "No. It's something we need to work out for ourselves."

Jo's eyes moistened. She could not believe she was becoming emotional. Kim, Sam, and Chrissy's happy home was the only stable thing in Jo's life. She could always rely on her brother, sister-in-law, and niece for support. Whenever she was having a horrible day, just knowing she could go and spend an evening with them gave her hope.

"Don't be like that, darling," Kim said, giving Jo a motherly hug.

"I love you guys so much."

"And we love you, Jo," Kim said, wiping tears from Jo's eyes.

"Is it because of me?" Jo asked. Sam was always concerned for her well-being. Was she a thorn in their relationship?

"Don't be silly," Kim said. "Sometimes, people start moving apart."

"But, you guys are so happy together."

"Well, that's what all couples want other people to see."

"I didn't know it was this bad," Jo said.

"I didn't think so either. But the last month has not been very good. We hardly ever talk anymore."

"Have you thought about how this might affect Chrissy?"

"It's what's keeping me from taking the next step."

Jo looked Kim in the eye. "I want you to be happy. I want Sam to be happy. But promise me something."

"What?"

"Promise me that you'll think this through before you do anything and that you'll at least talk to Sam first. If, in the end, you still decide to separate, I'll be there to support you guys in any way I can."

Kim smiled. "I promise."

# THIRTEEN

Rhodes drove up to the trailer home and parked his Malibu. A large American flag flew from the roof of the trailer, a peace sign hung from one of the trailer's windows, and a Confederate flag was next to the symbol.

The words RHODES TO FREEDOM were painted in big block letters on one side of the trailer. The words were not there the last time Rhodes had visited. It was his father's moniker, and he printed it on everything he owned. The moniker used to be on his Harley Davidson until he had to sell it because he owed money to the wrong people.

Rhodes walked up and pounded on the front door.

A few seconds later, the door swung open, and out came Sullivan "Sully" Rhodes. Sully had on a brown leather jacket, blue jeans, and black boots. His head was not covered in his trademark bandana. Instead, his bald scalp was on full display. His bushy beard was white but flecked with nicotine.

"I came as fast as I could," Rhodes said. "Is everything okay?"

Rhodes still did not have a cell phone. He thought about getting one but decided against it. He did not have many people he needed to contact. Plus, he did not want anyone contacting him. If he wanted to make a call, he used the pay phone down the block from his apartment.

But Tess had a cell phone. What teenager did not these days? She told him that his father had called her and wanted Rhodes to come over immediately.

Rhodes was not sure how his father ~~had~~ ~~gotten~~ her number. Regardless, he was there now.

Sully smiled. "Yeah, everything is fine. You wanna come in, Marty?"

Rhodes frowned. "Tess told me it was an emergency."

"It is."

"Tell me."

"Outside?"

"Yes."

"Okay, but you sure you don't want a beer or anything?"

Ever since Rhodes saved Sully's life at the water plant, Sully had been acting extra nice to him. It was as if somehow the ocean-like gap between them had shortened, but it had not. Rhodes did not feel any differently. Sully was in danger and Rhodes did what he had to do, and that was the end of the matter.

There were moments, however, when Rhodes wished he had arrived late and Mathias Lotta had put Sully out of his misery. Rhodes was sure only a few people would miss him. He sure would not, but he had his reasons.

Some people should never have ~~gotten~~ married nor had any children. Sully was one of them. He had spent much of his life being selfish. He gambled, drank, and womanized with no care in the world. He never knew what it meant to be a good husband and father.

As a husband, he did not know that he should not cheat on his wife. As a father, he did not know he needed to provide for his child.

He did something not because he believed it was the right thing to do; he did it because that was what you were supposed to do. For instance, if you get a girl pregnant, you married her.

That was what happened with Sully.

Margaret "Maggie" Rhodes was far better than Sully in every way. She was smart, somewhat educated (she did go to college but dropped out before graduating), and she knew what it meant to be a wife and mother.

She did everything she could to hold her family together. If Sully was not working, she took any job to pay the bills. If Sully was drunk, she would take the brunt of his abuse so that it never reached her young son. If Sully disappeared for days, she made sure her son was never without anything.

Rhodes loved his mother more than any person he had ever loved. But she was flawed too. Her biggest mistake was getting involved with someone like Sully. She could have had any man. She was beautiful and vibrant, and men fawned over her. Instead, she chose Sully. Maybe it was his unpredictable nature that attracted her to him. She always said the time she spent with him may not have been stable or secure, but it was filled with a lot of fun and excitement.

She was probably looking for an escape from the mundane and tedious. Sully took her to a world that was anything but that.

She also always said the reason she chose to marry Sully was because of Rhodes. Rhodes hated hearing this from her. It was as if *he* was to blame for the way her life had ended up, even though he knew he was blameless. She could have left Sully, taking her young son and started a life someplace else. She did not, and Rhodes had to endure a tough childhood that involved beatings from his father and a path to a life of crime.

It was only after Maggie had passed away from cancer that Rhodes decided to change his life and start fresh. He wished she had still been alive so that she could see him become a police officer. But then she would have also seen him go to prison for murder. He knew that above everything else, this would have destroyed her. No mother wants to see her child end up behind bars.

"No, I don't want a beer," Rhodes said curtly. "Tell me why I'm here, or else the next time you choose to contact me and there is an actual emergency, I won't be nice enough to show up."

Sully looked down at his feet and adjusted his pants. "Yeah, sure, I'll get to the point. The thing is, after what happened with that guy knocking me out and pointing a gun to my head, it got me thinking, you know? I've made a lot of mistakes in life, with you, your mom, and with so many other people. And I realize now I don't want to die alone." He took a deep breath. "So, I've asked Patti to marry me."

Patti was Sully's girlfriend. Rhodes had always found it fascinating that someone like Sully, a man who never held a stable job in his life, was able to find women interested in him.

Rhodes thought for a moment before he asked, "Why're you telling me this?"

"I am telling you because I want you to be my best man."

Rhodes was dumbstruck. He gritted his teeth. "Why would I want to be your best man?"

"I mean, why not?" Sully asked, sounding irritated. "You're my son, after all."

Rhodes felt ready to lecture Sully about what it meant to be a father, but he held his tongue. He was not in the mood to get into an argument with the old man.

Sully read his son's face. He said in a low voice, "I know, things are never gonna be perfect between us, but Marty, I would love to have you stand next to me. It would mean the world to me if you did."

Rhodes stared at him. "I'll think about it," he finally said before he left.

# FOURTEEN

The FBI Bridgeton field office was located right in the middle of the city's downtown core. The concrete and granite building was a nightmare to get to during rush hour. In case of emergency, Jo could put her FBI-issued, flashing red light on her roof, but she reserved that for when there were no other options. So far, she only had to use it once. It was when a shooter had decided to storm a library and take everyone inside hostage. Apparently, the shooter was not happy with the fines the library had charged him for overdue materials and wanted them waived. The shooter was a schizophrenic who had stopped taking his medications.

Jo parked her Jetta in the underground parking of a nearby hotel and walked the rest of the way to the FBI building. She took the elevator to the sixth floor. The moment she got off, she was bombarded by a dozen voices.

Chris Foster, the FBI's IT specialist, was standing by Jo's desk. He wore a hoodie, cargo pants, and thick socks with sandals. He also sported a mushroom haircut. "One date," he said. "That's all I'm asking for."

Next to him was Special Agent Irina Januska. She had on a tight blouse with a leather jacket over it. Her dark hair was tied in a ponytail, and she was in great physical shape. Irina was preparing to try out for the American Sports Challenge, where men and women raced through extreme obstacle courses in order to win a million dollars. So far, though, she had not made it to the competition.

"I gave you a chance," she said in her Eastern European accent. "If you'd completed the challenge, I would've gone out on a date with you."

"That entire competition wasn't fair, to begin with," Chris complained. "You work out every day. Plus, you train on those difficult courses twice a week. The last time I was at the gym, I was in high school, and I only did it to get a credit."

Jo shook her head. Chris had been after Irina to go out with him for a long time. It felt like either he was too stubborn or that he just did not get that she was not interested in him. Or perhaps he was hoping to wear her down. Maybe one day, she would get tired of him and just give in.

"Why do you have to discuss this by my desk?" Jo asked.

Chris shrugged. "It was empty, so we figured it would be a great place to discuss our situation."

"We don't have a situation," Irina said. "And we didn't choose to discuss anything. He just cornered me on my way to the ladies' room."

Chris smiled. "And I will let you be on your way if you agree to a date with yours truly."

"I could just hurt you," Irina said, crossing her arms over her chest. "It wouldn't be difficult to break your fingers or your arms."

"That's a direct threat," Chris said, turning to Jo. "And you're my witness."

Jo sighed. She suddenly realized it was not just Irina who was tired of hearing this. She, too, had had enough. She said to Chris, "If Irina goes out with you, will you stop asking her out?"

"Hey, wait a minute…" Irina said.

"Will you?" Jo quickly asked.

Chris shrugged. "Sure."

Jo turned to Irina. "Do you like that he asks you out all the time?"

"No. It's annoying."

"Then go out with him this *one* time. If after that, he asks you out again, I'll personally shoot him in the legs and tell Walters he was high on drugs and needed to be subdued."

Chris's mouth dropped.

Irina smiled. "I like the sound of that."

"But…" Chris stammered.

"I'll do it," Irina said.

"But…"

"Then that's it," Jo said. "One date, and then we'll never hear another word about it."

A man walked over. Special Agent Tarik Habib was tall, well-built, and had tanned skin and brown eyes. "What's with all the smiles?" he asked.

"Irina has agreed to go out with Chris," Jo answered.

"Hey, that's great news." Tarik looked at Chris. "Why don't you look happy?"

He swallowed. "I'm smiling on the inside."

Jo smiled. "Do you have photos to share, Tarik?"

"As promised," Tarik replied, holding out photos of his one-month-old daughter.

After Crowder's death, a dark cloud had hung over the unit. The birth of a child had brightened up the team's mood. Tarik and his wife had named their daughter Sophia. Ever since she had been born, he was beaming like a proud papa.

Jo said, "You should take some time off, you know."

"I will, but not right now," Tarik replied. "My mother-in-law is here from Kansas, and the last thing I want is to be stuck at home with her."

"It might not be all bad," Irina said. "You might like her once you get to know her."

"I doubt that."

Chris held up the baby photos. "I'm glad she looks like your wife. Your wife is hot."

Tarik gave him a look.

Chris swallowed again. "I didn't mean it like that. I think all women look hot."

Walters stuck her head out of her office. "Jo! Can I see you for a minute?" she yelled out.

The group quickly dispersed.

Jo walked over and took a seat across from Walter's desk. "What's going on?" Jo asked.

"We need to talk."

"About what?"

"It's Crowder's wife. She wants to sue the Bureau for his death."

"What?" Jo exclaimed. "Why?"

"She blames us for what happened."

"We didn't kill Crowder, Mathias Lotta did."

"Yes, but you were dating Mathias. Crowder's wife thinks your relationship put Crowder's life in danger."

"We never discussed any ongoing investigations," Jo said. "Plus, wasn't she going to leave Crowder anyway? Why is she suddenly playing the mournful widow?"

"Money. What else?" Walters replied. "If her lawyers can find a way to prove that we were negligent in any way, we could be held responsible for his demise. If that happens, his survivor benefits could triple."

"Crowder died in the line of duty. His wife received substantial compensation."

"True, but if she could get more, then she's willing to take her chances. So, I want to be sure that no information was ever passed on to Mathias."

Jo thought for a moment. "During our relationship, I had no idea who he was," she said. "I can assure you that I would never willingly do anything or say anything that would jeopardize the safety and well-being of a fellow officer."

Walters stared at Jo. "You can go," she said a minute later.

# FIFTEEN

Rhodes was going through the file Mac had given him when he heard yelling from upstairs. It was in Russian, but Rhodes did not need to speak the language to know what the commotion was about. Ever since his landlady's son had returned from prison, both mother and son were at each other's throats.

The son's name was Yevgeny. Rhodes knew this because he had heard his landlady say it over a dozen times whenever she and her son fought.

Yevgeny had served six months for grand theft auto. He and his buddies were involved in stealing luxury cars and selling them to chop shops. By the time the police had begun their search for the stolen vehicle, its parts would have already been shipped to various countries around the world.

Yevgeny would not have been caught had he not gotten cocky. He was in the process of jacking a Ferrari from someone's private garage when he spotted a classic Aston Martin. He decided he wanted that vehicle instead. What he did not realize was that the Aston Martin had been loaned to the individual by a local car dealer. The police tracked the vehicle from the moment Yevgeny drove the car away. Instead of driving straight to the chop shop, he drove the car home to show it to his mother. His mother was surprised to see such a rare vehicle in her son's possession. She was even more surprised when her house was raided by the police a few minutes later. They took Yevgeny away, kicking and screaming in front of his crying mother.

He only received a six-month sentence because all he could be charged with was the theft of the Aston Martin. His decision not to go to the chop shop had saved him many years behind bars. Had he gone to the shop first, the police would have infiltrated a multi-country car theft ring.

Rhodes knew all this because the moment the son had appeared, Rhodes had done some digging. He wanted to know if the son would be trouble or not. Tess lived just above them, and the last thing Rhodes wanted was for her to get involved in something that she could not get herself out of.

Rhodes had not yet met Yevgeny. He only knew him from his research.

Rhodes could hear some English mixed in with the Russian and gleaned that Yevgeny was back with his old gang. His mother was not too pleased. She wanted him to get an honest job instead of risking going back to prison.

Silence suddenly descended upstairs, followed by the slamming of a door.

Rhodes stood up and walked over to the window. Outside, two men were standing next to a shiny Cadillac. Yevgeny walked up to them, exchanged handshakes, and got in the Cadillac.

Rhodes shook his head. He was glad he did not have any children. He did not know how he would deal with them if they were like Yevgeny. Also, he was a convicted felon and his father was a career criminal, so his children would not have to look far to see what kind of life lay ahead of them.

Rhodes was back to reading the file when there was a knock at the door. He opened it and found his landlady standing before him. She was a heavyset woman. She had on a colorful sweatshirt, and her short blonde hair was tied in a ponytail.

Her name was Olya, and even after being a tenant of hers for several months, Rhodes still did not know her last name. He did not need to. He always paid her in cash, so he never had to write her a check.

"Mr. Rose," she said. He was certain she was saying 'Rhodes', but in her heavy accent, it sounded like *rose*. "I need your help."

He could see she had been crying.

"What can I do for you?" Rhodes asked, feeling a bit hesitant about possibly getting involved in her family dispute.

"Mr. Rose, you have to talk to Yevgeny. You have to make him leave the bad people he hangs around with."

Rhodes sighed. "I'm not sure how I can do that."

"You were a police officer before, yes?"

"A detective…"

"Then you can make him listen to you," Olya said. "I try to talk to him, but it does not work. If he doesn't change, he will end up like his father."

"Your husband was in prison?" Rhodes asked.

"He still is, in Russia. He did things for very bad people. He killed too many people."

*He was a hitman or an enforcer*, Rhodes thought.

Olya said, "I came to this country to give my son a better life, and now he is doing bad things."

71

She broke into loud sobs. Rhodes did not know what to do, but Olya quickly composed herself, wiping her eyes with the back of her sleeve.

"Please, Mr. Rose. I don't want my son to be like his father."

Rhodes grimaced. He knew what it was like to have a father who was nothing but a negative influence.

He sighed again. "All right, I'll see what I can do."

## SIXTEEN

When Jo received the call, she was at the scene in a matter of minutes.

She found Tarik standing before a cargo van. The van had been left by the side of the road behind a group of trees, rendering the vehicle almost invisible.

The license plate was missing.

"How'd they find it?" Jo asked.

"That guy over there called it in," Tarik replied, nodding in the direction of a man wearing a checkered shirt, a large vest, and a trucker's cap. The man was standing next to a station wagon. "He's from out of state, visiting his sister. After a long drive, he stopped by the side of the road to take a leak when he noticed the van. He thought maybe someone had had an accident or maybe someone had left it. He figured he'd quickly strip it for parts. He's a mechanic if that helps. Anyway, when he went over to the van, that's when he saw this."

Tarik took her to the back of the van. He pointed to a spot by the edge of the back door. Tarik did not need to tell her what it was. Blood was dripping through the crack and falling on the grass below. There was already a red puddle.

Jo nodded as two officers reached for the door handles. She braced herself as they carefully opened the van door.

She was relieved to find no one inside. She feared another dead body. But there was something in the middle of the van. It was a large black bucket. When the officers pulled the bucket out, they found more dark liquid inside it. *That explains the blood*, she thought.

Then another thought occurred to her. Ben was right. The killer had drained his victim's blood. And he had used the back of the van as his kill room.

If that was true, this blood belonged to George Moll.

The forensics team would take the van into the lab and examine it thoroughly. Jo doubted that they would find anything useful, however. The killer had been careful.

Just then, she heard Tarik's voice cry, "Jo!"

She spotted him twenty feet away.

She walked over and found him kneeling. He was pointing to what looked like tire tracks.

"How do you suppose those got there?" he asked.

Jo knew exactly how. The killer had not abandoned the van here randomly. He had chosen this location for its obscurity. Once he had disposed of the van, he had driven away in another vehicle.

A feeling of unease swept over her. She realized they were no closer to solving this case. In fact, they now had more questions than answers.

# SEVENTEEN

Jo entered the lobby of the FBI building. Her face turned grim when she saw Dr. Ansel Lotta waiting for her.

Lotta had thick white hair and gray eyes. His skin had taken on a leathery texture from years spent sailing the world. For a man his age, he was in excellent shape. His hands were strong and sturdy, which was an asset in his line of work as a surgeon.

Jo knew a lot about him because he was Mathias's father.

Jo crossed her arms. "What can I do for you, Dr. Lotta?" she asked, knowing full well why he was there.

"I'm surprised you'd even ask that question," he replied. "I would like to see my son."

"And like I've told you over and over again, that is not possible," Jo said.

Lotta gave her a hard look. "I will keep pushing for it, and so will my lawyers."

"You're wasting your time and your money. Mathias is under a criminal investigation, and until then, we decide who he sees and who he doesn't."

"He's my son, and I have every right to see him."

"You should've thought of that before you shot him."

Lotta sighed. "I realize what I did may have been overzealous. But you have to realize he had threatened to harm me and my family. You were there at my house that night to stop him from doing just that. Plus, it was you who took me to that water facility in order to barter me for your friend's father."

"I would have never given you up," Jo said. "Your son demanded we bring you or else he would've killed another person. You were only there to buy us time."

"Time for what?" Lotta asked in a hard tone. "He had a gun and he was going to use it on us."

"You did too," Jo said, almost raising her voice.

"What choice did I have?" he said. "I wasn't going to go into a situation without being armed. It was for my protection. And you can't blame me for being cautious considering the threat I was under."

"Might I remind you, Dr. Lotta," Jo said, "that right now, your son is the one under constant threat. There was already an attempt on his life. It is for that reason we have to be extra vigilant in who we allow near him."

Lotta said in a calm tone, "I want only what is best for my son."

"Apparently, that's not what he wanted for you."

"Why are you making this so difficult?" he demanded. "Why won't you give me access to him? Is it because you still have feelings for him?"

Jo did not reply.

"Might I remind *you*, Special Agent Pullinger, that my son murdered several people in cold blood. If you think you are protecting him by stopping me from seeing him, you are wrong. It is you and I who need protection from him."

Jo said, "I'm not protecting Mathias. I'm protecting the information he possesses. At the water facility, he was going to tell us something, and you prevented that from happening. You are lucky we didn't charge you for attempted murder."

Lotta's lips curled into an arrogant smirk. "Go ahead. Charge me for stopping a killer. I did what you couldn't do. You should have shot him the moment you had the chance."

"I thought you were concerned about your son's well-being?"

"I am also concerned about other people's well-being," Lotta said. "My son has done a lot of harm, but as his father, I know there is good in him. I have to believe this, which is why I want to help him. I can't do that if I can't see him."

"Your son wanted you dead. I think you're the last person he'd want to see. Plus, I'm curious to know what you did that made him want to kill you."

Lotta was silent for a moment. "My son and I have had our differences," he said. His tone was slow and even. "I'm sure he feels that I have hurt him in the past. That is why I want to make it up to him now. The last time I saw him was at the Bridgeton Mental Care Institute. And before you say that I put him there, I will repeat that I had no choice. My life and my family's lives were in danger. I had hoped by getting him the proper care, he'd get better, and I could bring him back into my life. Instead, he turned into a vengeful killer. This, I assure you, I never imagined would ever happen." He paused as if taking a deep breath. "All I'm asking is that you let me see Mathias."

Jo stared at him. "The moment your son wakes up and tells us what we want to know, we'll give you a call."

She walked to the elevators.

# EIGHTEEN

Rhodes sat in his Malibu. It was parked outside his apartment. He preferred the inside of the car because the apartment was not conducive to rumination. There were too many distractions in the old house. There was noise from the water pipes, the stomping of feet from upstairs, the occasional slamming of doors, and the roaring of the outdated furnace. Not to mention Olya's arguments with Yevgeny.

Rhodes was still unsure about how to get Yevgeny on the right track, but he would deal with it when the time came. At the moment, he needed to find a solution to the case Mac had dropped on his lap.

Rhodes pinched the top of his nose. There was so much on his plate right now: Mac's investigation, his landlady's request for help, his father's desire for him to be his best man, and the matter of Mathias Lotta.

It was Dr. Ansel Lotta who had hired Rhodes to find his son. At first, Rhodes was not sure why when all the evidence showed Mathias had died in a car accident. But the body had been burned beyond recognition. This had cast doubt as to whether he was in the car when it had gone up in flames. There was more to this story than he could put his finger on, but that too would have to wait.

Mac's case was perplexing. He was certain Adam Channing had murdered Myron and Jenny Goldsmith. Adam was devastated when Jenny had broken up with him. He was obsessed to the point that he knew everything about her life. He was a stalker who had the means and motive to commit the murder. But then there was his airtight alibi. Adam was at a concert with his friend on the night Jenny was murdered. In fact, several people—including the security guards—confirmed seeing him enter and leave.

How was that possible if he was across town stabbing Myron and Jenny Goldsmith?

Rhodes took a deep breath. *What if Mac is wrong?* he thought. *What if Adam Channing did not commit the crime? What if Mac is so obsessed with finding the killer that he could not look beyond someone who seemed suspicious, and all because his daughter was friends with Jenny?*

Rhodes shook his head. He was not sure if Mac was right or wrong regarding Adam Channing. But Rhodes would do his due diligence and give his opinion on the case, even if it ended up being against what Mac wanted to hear.

Maybe the case had become too personal for Mac. Rhodes had made the same mistake before, and it ended up costing him his freedom, marriage, and career. Maybe it was a good thing Mac had come to him for help. Rhodes was neutral on Adam's guilt. All he cared about were the facts. If they proved Adam's innocence, Rhodes would make sure no harm came to him.

A suspect's potential innocence had always kept Rhodes up at night. He feared to put someone in prison for a crime they never committed. Letting a murderer walk free was worse than locking up an innocent man. This was why he always made sure to double-check the evidence. If there was even a hint of doubt, he would hold off before charging someone.

During Rhodes's time in prison, he had sometimes wondered, *What if I was innocent but still got locked up? God, I'd feel miserable, especially if the perpetrator who did the crime got to roam free while I suffered in jail.*

No. Rhodes would not rush into judgment. He would follow the evidence and see where it led.

A car pulled up behind him. He watched through the rearview mirror as Mac got out.

He walked over and tapped on the window. Rhodes lowered it. Mac handed Rhodes an envelope. "Let me know what you find," Mac said.

As Mac left, Rhodes opened the envelope and pulled out a DVD.

It was the security footage from the concert.

## NINETEEN

Rhodes was still in his car when Tess slid into the passenger seat. "Why are you sitting in your car?" she asked.

"I was thinking," he replied.

She made a face. "You can do that in your apartment, you know. I go to the library. It's quiet and no one bothers you."

Rhodes sighed. "I was also waiting for you."

Rhodes could have walked up to the third floor and knocked on the door, but he wanted to avoid meeting Tess's mom.

Rhodes and Tess's mom had not gotten off on the right foot. It started when Tess accused her mom's ex-boyfriend of being a creep. Rhodes normally hated intervening, but on this occasion, he had stood up for Tess. The boyfriend was eventually booted out of the house. Her mom was not seeing anyone at the moment, though. If she was, Tess would have mentioned it to him.

He was not sure why he even cared. It was not like it was any of his business. He was just a neighbor.

But Rhodes was fond of Tess. He wanted nothing but the best for her. She was smart, had a good head on her shoulders, and was far more responsible than any teenager he knew. If she had someone to guide her, he believed she could do great things in her life.

Rhodes did not know how long he would stay in his current apartment. It was too cramped for a man his size. Several times a day, he would hit his head either on the door, the air ducts, or the bathroom shower head.

With all the bumps and bruises he had accumulated, he should have moved out months ago. But again, it came down to Tess.

By moving away, he would feel like he was abandoning her, something her father had done when she was young.

He knew he was too emotional about it. Tess was nothing to him but a friend. Also, what could he do if her mom suddenly decided to move out? He knew she worked at a nail salon. What if she got laid off and had to relocate to find work? He would have stuck around for nothing.

"So, why were you waiting for me?" Tess asked.

"I need you to do something for me," Rhodes replied.

"Like what?"

"I've got a new case."

"Yippee!" Tess squealed in excitement.

Rhodes had unofficially hired Tess as his assistant. It was not full-time, but only when he needed her help.

"I don't have a computer," Rhodes said. "I want you to go through this security camera footage and tell me if you see anything unusual."

Rhodes held out the DVD for her. Tess took it and said, "What am I looking for?"

"Not what, but who," Rhodes handed her a photo of Adam Channing. It was from the file Mac had given him.

"Who is he?" she asked, examining the photo. It was a black-and-white mug shot of Adam from two years ago, taken when he had been arrested for an assault outside a bar. In the photo, Adam had short hair, a goatee, an earring in his left ear, and a crooked smile.

"His name is Adam Channing, and he's a suspect in a murder investigation," Rhodes said.

"That's so cool," Tess said with a big smile.

Rhodes always forgot how young she was. To someone like her, everything was either cool or not cool.

"He will be accompanied by another man. It's his friend. I want you to see if he or his friend ever left the venue during the concert."

"Do you have a photo of the friend?" she asked. "I mean, how would I know what he looks like."

Rhodes opened his mouth but then shut it. He had not asked Mac for one. Why would he? The friend was not a suspect; Adam was. But Tess had a legitimate concern. "The friend should be with the suspect," Rhodes said. "They both had tickets to the concert. You spot the suspect, and you'll spot the friend."

"Gotcha," she said, putting the DVD in her backpack. "Okay, I'll play it on my laptop and let you know what I find."

# TWENTY

The sun was at its peak as Jo jogged along the side of the street. It was midafternoon, and there was not a cloud in the sky. The weather was also cool, so it was a perfect day to be outside.

Jo was dressed in a green tracksuit and yellow runners. She had earbuds in her ears, but no music was playing on her smartphone. She was using her earbuds only as earplugs today. Jo had stopped going to the gym. She had met Mathias there. He had approached her first, but she had rebuffed him. He was relentless until she finally agreed to go out with him. She thought he was nice, and he looked harmless. After all, he was a professor at a local college. Plus, there was something else that attracted her to him: He was interested in the Bridgeton Ripper case. The Ripper had become an obsession of hers. She wanted nothing more than to find the person responsible for her father's death.

It was only later that she realized why Mathias was so interested in the case. His mother, Annabelle Burton, was one of the Ripper's victims.

Maybe he and she were not so different. They both wanted to solve their parent's murders, and they both felt neglected growing up. After her father died, her mother was a wreck, and in her grief, she had pushed her daughter away. She was depressed most of the days and was not really there for Jo and Sam. It was their maternal grandparents who had stepped in and raised them.

After Mathias's mother was killed, it was his father who had pushed him away, locking him up in a mental institute. His father had remarried by then and started a family. How difficult it must have been for Mathias to see that his father had moved on and he had not—or could not. He probably looked at his father as a protective figure, and when he could not protect his mother, he lashed out at him and his new family.

Jo was not sure if that was actually the case. Mathias could have been a troubled child to begin with, having psychopathic tendencies at a very young age.

And that was where their similarities ended.

Mathias had killed many people in cold blood, including a policeman. In this regard, she and Mathias were on opposite ends of the spectrum.

Jo jogged through an alley, taking a shortcut to another street.

She checked her smartwatch. She had been running for twenty minutes. If she was on a treadmill, she would have already broken into a sweat.

Her heart condition had not gotten any better. In fact, lately, her condition had gotten worse. The pain came more frequently and stayed longer. She felt that by jogging, she would strengthen her heart.

As she moved over a bridge, she felt much better about herself. She knew it was the endorphins kicking in, but she did not care. She did not want the feeling to go away. After months of feeling down about what happened with Mathias and Crowder, it was good to let positivity flow into her mind and body.

She spotted a path and took it. The path was long and winding, stretching the entire length of a park.

She checked her pulse and it was steady.

She jogged around a playground, and she thought of Chrissy. She should bring her to the park and play with her. Chrissy was only five, but in a few years, she may not want to hang around with Jo, and Jo would miss these precious moments she could have spent with her.

Suddenly, she felt a sharp pain and clutched at her chest. The pain was powerful and overwhelming. She felt dizzy, and her knees buckled underneath her. She dropped to the ground and nearly hit her head on the concrete.

She looked up and the sun blinded her.

Jo heard a dog barking. A woman then came into her view. "Are you okay?" she asked.

Jo blinked. She was drenched in sweat.

"I'm going to lift you up," the woman said.

Jo nodded.

She grabbed Jo under her arms and helped her to a nearby bench. She offered Jo water from her bottle. Jo took it and took a big drink.

"Thank you," Jo said, giving the woman a weak smile.

"Are you okay?" the woman asked.

"I'm fine," Jo replied.

But she was not, and she knew why.

# TWENTY-ONE

Jo was in a small office. She had been there before, and she did not mind waiting. She stared out the window and could see Bridgeton Harbor in the distance. As always, she wished she was there instead, but what happened earlier scared her. She was not sure why. Maybe it was because she was not ready to die.

Normally, death did not terrify her. She had seen too many dead bodies to not accept it as part of life. She knew her time would come, and in some ways, she was prepared for death. That day was different.

With Mathias in a coma and with her brother and sister-in-law on the verge of separation, she did not want to die. There were still so many unresolved issues. What was it that Mathias wanted to tell her at the water facility? What would happen to Chrissy if Sam and Kim decided to divorce? Then there was still the matter of her mother. Even in her current condition, she deserved to know who had murdered her husband.

Jo was not sure if the latter would ever happen in her lifetime. She had already spent years digging into the Bridgeton Ripper case with no success. She was not sure what would change that now.

The door swung open and a man came in wearing a white lab coat. Dr. Jacob Cohen was short, bald, and his beard had long ago turned gray. Dr. Cohen was the lead medical specialist at Bridgeton Mercy Hospital. He had also been good friends with Jo's father.

"Sorry for keeping you waiting," Dr. Cohen said, walking around and sitting behind his desk. "We had a medical emergency."

Jo nodded. She was grateful Dr. Cohen always managed to spare some time for her in his busy schedule.

He removed his glasses and pinched the top of his thin nose. "When did you experience the pain?"

"When I was out jogging earlier."

"Where?"

"In my chest."

After several more questions, Dr. Cohen said, "Why are you here, Jo?"

Jo looked at him. She was confused. "I thought you said I should come right away if I felt severe pain. I did today."

"And I also told you numerous times that your condition will only get better if you get a heart transplant."

Jo looked away, staring out the window.

"Jo," Dr. Cohen said. "I know you've got a lot going on in your life. I heard about the murders, but they are not your responsibility. Your responsibility is to get better, and in order to do that, we need to get you on a transplant list."

Jo shook her head. "Not right now."

"Then when?"

She looked down at her hands. "Soon."

"And when will that be?"

"I don't know."

"The longer you wait, the worse your condition will become. I fear even a transplant might not do any good if we delay the procedure."

Jo did not say anything.

Dr. Cohen sighed. "If you won't listen to me about getting the transplant, then at least listen to me and get some rest."

"I will. I promise. But not right now," Jo said.

Dr. Cohen's face hardened, his steely gray eyes locking onto her. Jo almost felt like they were burning into her soul.

"You tried doing it your way," Dr. Cohen said. You exercised, you changed your diet, but in the end, your problem is still there."

Jo just looked at him.

"Under normal circumstances, I don't force my patients to do anything they don't want to, but in your case, I will make an exception. As your physician, I am ordering you to take some time off and rest."

"I appreciate your concern, Dr. Cohen, but I don't think you have the authority to make me do that."

Dr. Cohen leaned back in his chair. A grin crossed his face. "I hope I don't have to remind you that all law enforcement personnel have to pass a medical examination every three years. Unless they get a clearance certificate stating they are fit to perform their duties, they are suspended until they receive such a certificate. From your file, I can see your three years are almost up. If you want, I can schedule a full examination." He put his glasses on and made a show of checking his calendar. "I can schedule you in next week. I'm sure you will get a clean bill of health."

She knew what he was doing. If she did not agree to voluntarily take time off, he would force her to do so.

Dr. Cohen put his hands together and looked directly into her eyes. He gave her a reassuring smile. "Jo, I've known you since you had braces. I know how dedicated you are to your job, which was why three years ago, I gave you a pass under the condition that you come every month to get your heart checked."

"And I've never missed an appointment, Dr. Cohen," Jo said.

"I know, but your condition is only getting worse, not better. Don't make me do something I don't want to."

Jo looked down at her feet. She felt like a kid being lectured by her teacher.

She knew he was right. The pressure had been intense in the last few months. There was the stress of Mathias and her relationship with him. Then Crowder's death had devastated her. On top of that, Dr. Lotta was relentless in harassing her to let him see his son. And then there was Walters, who was also constantly on her back to take a break.

Dr. Cohen said, "Jo, go home and get some rest, even if it's only for a few days. Believe me. It'll do wonders for not only your heart but your overall health as well."

She finally nodded.

## TWENTY-TWO

Rhodes pulled his Malibu to a stop by the side of the street. He turned off the engine and watched the automobile garage across from him.

For the better part of the day, Rhodes had been following Yevgeny, starting when two of his buddies picked him up. They drove straight from the apartment house to a nearby liquor store, and from there, they had headed to a dry cleaner, where they disappeared into the back for an hour.

They had then driven around some nicer neighborhoods. Every once in a while, the Cadillac would slow down as they looked at a Bently parked in a driveway, or a BMW parked on the street, or a Tesla parked inside an open garage.

Rhodes knew exactly what they were up to. They were scoping out their next targets. Even after spending six months in jail, Yevgeny was back to stealing cars with his buddies.

This time, they were more careful. On a number of occasions, either Yevgeny or one of his buddies would get out of the Cadillac, walk up to a vehicle, look around to see if anyone was looking, and then mark X on all four tires with a piece of chalk.

This was their way of keeping tabs on the vehicle. They would return later in the day or the next day and see if the same vehicle was parked in the same spot. If it was, they would know when and where to strike.

Rhodes could not tell if the markings were made for someone else. What if Yevgeny and his buddies were spotters, and others came in and did the job? There was no way to know unless he saw someone jack a vehicle, but he did not have time to follow Yevgeny until he did something like that. There were other, more urgent matters that needed Rhodes's attention.

He checked his watch. He was not sure how long Yevgeny and his buddies intended to stay in the garage. He could not wait all day.

*I should come back tomorrow*, he thought. *Maybe follow Yevgeny around the city again and see what they are up to then.*

As he was about to start the engine, Rhodes spotted a vehicle in the distance. Rhodes was not sure why he had not seen it before. It was a black Ford Crown Victoria. It was unmarked, but Rhodes knew the two men seated inside were undercover police officers.

They were wearing suits and ties, and one of them had on sunglasses. The other was busy taking a drink through a straw.

*Idiots*, Rhodes thought. *Don't you realize you stick out like sore thumbs?*

His brow furrowed. Maybe that was the point. Maybe they wanted the car thieves to know they were being watched.

It was a strategy he was familiar with. The police would make it look like their focus was on the one location. Meanwhile, they were also keeping an eye on everyone involved. The criminals would become guarded, and instead of using the one location, they would start using others, ones they did not think the police were aware of.

The police knew the garage across the street was being used as a chop shop. Stolen vehicles were brought in to be disassembled so that their parts could be sold separately. In some cases, if the gang was also involved in drugs, which most were, then the parts would be used to smuggle drugs into other countries. It was not uncommon for border police to confiscate crates of carburetors, radiators, and mufflers that were stuffed with cocaine.

Rhodes was not sure how big or far-reaching Yevgeny's gang was, but the police felt they were enough of a threat to allocate resources to them.

Olya was right to worry that sooner or later, her son would end up back in prison. It was a matter of time before the police got the order, and the garage would be swarming with officers.

Rhodes had to do something if he wanted to help his landlady. *But what?* he thought.

Rhodes frowned and rubbed his chin. He knew he could not let Yevgeny throw his life away. He had seen too many young people end up in prison. Some were proud of their actions. They wanted "street cred," and nothing was better than spending time behind bars. Others regretted the position they were in. They only committed the crime because there was nothing else for them to do. They did not have a good education, and their job prospects were bleak. Crime was the only way they knew how to make a living. These penitent convicts talked to Rhodes because he was not only a former police officer but also one of them. Plus, there were not many people in prison who would listen to their tales of sorrow. Most of the prisoners had been raised in the same environment and thus accepted the position they were in.

Rhodes was different. Although he had grown up surrounded by crime, he had made a good life for himself. He was a well-respected detective with a bright future ahead of him. He had seen the other side of the law. He could not say the same for many of the young men locked up in prison. Most would always be on the wrong side of the law, no matter what.

Rhodes took a deep breath. He wanted to stop that from happening to Yevgeny.

The garage's front door opened, and Yevgeny and his buddies came out. One of them lit a cigarette and took a long drag. He then handed it to Yevgeny, who took a long drag as well.

Suddenly, Rhodes had an idea.

He put the Chevy in gear and drove up to the garage. He drove past the men smoking in front and yelled, "Yevgeny! I'll see you later!"

He drove away. In the rearview mirror, he could see Yevgeny was puzzled by what had just happened.

Rhodes knew exactly what he was doing.

## TWENTY-THREE

Jo hated being at home, but she had no choice. When she told Walters she was taking some time off, she could almost hear the SAC's sigh of relief. Walters had been pushing Jo to take a break. She was one of the few people who knew of Jo's heart condition. She cared for Jo, even if she did not show it because of their working relationship.

There were many occasions where Walters had threatened to suspend Jo after another one of her health scares. But Jo was too valuable to the FBI, and Walters could not afford to be without one of her best agents.

Jo had hoped that would be the case now, too. Whenever she told Walters of her decision to take a leave of absence, Walters would hesitate and perhaps even request her to delay her leave. But that did not happen this time. Walters accepted Jo's decision the moment she told her. Maybe with Tarik and Irina taking on more responsibilities, Walters had enough good agents to keep the department moving. In an odd way, Jo kind of resented this. She wanted to be needed. Her job had become a big part of her life, defining who she was. Fortunately, she still had her FBI credentials and weapon. She was still an agent. She was only on a short leave.

She walked around the house. It was a mess. The kitchen sink was piled high with dirty dishes. The floor was sticky and needed a good mopping. There were cobwebs in the corner of the ceiling. The carpet in the bedrooms had not been vacuumed in weeks. Clothes were either on the bed or on the floor. The dirty laundry had been dumped in front of the closet. The bathroom was disgusting and stank. Jo could not believe she was comfortable using the bathroom. Maybe she did not care. *I will eventually get to it*, she kept telling herself. But that day always got pushed back.

She stopped in the living room and her shoulders sagged. The walls were plastered with magazine articles, newspaper clippings, police reports, photos of witnesses, and anything else that had to do with the Bridgeton Ripper case.

She took a deep breath. She had brought Mathias to her house. She had shared an aspect of her personal life with him that she had never shared with anyone. He seemed genuinely interested in the case. He knew as much about it as she did.

Her obsession had been a lonely one. Ben knew about it, and so did Sam, but no one was as intimately involved in it as she was. So, it was nice to see someone who shared her obsession. Mathias had claimed his master's thesis was on the Bridgeton Ripper. This was a lie. He had never gone to graduate school.

Everything about him had been false. He was not Pierre Picaud, the man she had fallen for. He was Mathias Lotta, a man who was out for revenge. He was not a professor at Cedar College who had a graduate degree in criminology. He was unemployed, living off a substantial trust fund. And he was not interested in a serial killer from decades before. He was a serial killer himself.

*How could I have been so wrong about him?* she wondered. *How could I have become so enamored with him so quickly?*

Mathias had used every means possible to get close to her. He knew her vulnerability, and he had taken advantage of it.

But there was more to him than just that.

She had sensed it when they were together. He was hiding something, and she had a feeling he had wanted to tell her the night he was shot. She could see it in his eyes and feel it in his voice.

If he had stripped her of her armor, she had done the same to him. They both had secrets. She had told him hers, but he never got the chance to tell her his.

She shook her head. There was no point in thinking about that now. There was no telling when or if Mathias would ever wake up.

She looked around the house and decided it was time to fix the place up. At least it would give her something to do, or else she would spend her time off mentally tormenting herself.

## TWENTY-FOUR

Amy Lange woke up to find her alarm buzzing. She hit the snooze button and went back to sleep. Five minutes later, the alarm woke her up again. This time, she hit the *off* button.

Amy worked for a privately funded center that helped victims of sexual violence. Amy never thought she would ever be involved in such a program. She always thought she would be traveling the world, performing with an orchestra.

Amy loved the cello. She started playing it when she was only four years old. It was introduced to her by her maternal grandfather. He was an immigrant from Hungary who had played with the Budapest Symphony Orchestra.

He was elated when his granddaughter showed a keen interest in the instrument. He died before Amy turned twelve, but he did live long enough to see her play alongside some of the brightest musical students in her home state.

Amy's father wanted her to get a real education. He was the owner of a successful shipping business and was averse to her going to music school. On the other hand, her mother wanted her daughter to follow her dreams.

After much debate, her parents came to a compromise. Amy would go to college and pursue a degree in business, and on the weekends and in the summer, her parents would pay for her to take classes at a prestigious music academy. This way, she would get an education that she could use in the real world and, at the same time, learn and be surrounded by the sounds of the cello.

Life was great for Amy until one fateful night. She was in her sophomore year when her friends pushed her to go to a frat party. Amy hesitated. She had heard terrible things about these parties. But her friends were persistent.

Amy did not have a boyfriend, and her friends wanted her to meet someone. They knew boys from various fraternities would be at this party. They hoped one of them would catch her eye.

Reluctantly, Amy agreed.

The party was at the house of one of the most popular students on campus. Kyle Summers was tall, handsome, and rated one of the top ten college football players in the state. There were rumors that he could one day play in the pros.

The university was promoting him heavily in all their televised football games. His face was everywhere on campus. Faculty members and students went out of their way to appease him. He could have chosen any university, and he had chosen theirs. He was their hero and their savior.

Amy had never met Kyle, but she knew about him.

The party was loud, and there were lots of people. There was also lots of booze. Amy was not a big drinker, but at her friends' insistence, she had drunk more than she could handle.

The next thing she remembered was waking up in a bedroom. She was undressed, and Kyle was nowhere to be found. But Amy knew something terrible had happened. She remembered him approaching her during the party and being nice to her. She also remembered being smitten by him. Then she remembered holding his hand as he took her upstairs to his bedroom.

She told her friends what happened, and they thought it was great she had hooked up with Kyle. But she told them it was not consensual. She could not remember anything.

She then went to one of her professors, who brought the matter up with the dean of the university. The dean was not convinced. He thought her memory of events was unreliable. She was drunk, after all. She later found out the dean was more concerned about how this would impact the millions the university received for their athletics program. If their star player got embroiled in a scandal, sponsors would be driven away in droves.

She was told to forget about Summers. She had no proof that anything had actually taken place that night. If she pursued the matter further, she was jeopardizing her academic career.

They had, in essence, muzzled her. She was afraid, and she went into a deep depression. She dropped out of the university and moved back in with her parents. She never spoke of the incident to them or anyone else again.

Kyle went on to play two more years at the university, but in his last game, he broke his leg. The injury was so severe that it required four separate operations for it to be restored. However, his prospects at playing pro football were gone.

The last she heard of him was that he had moved to Texas and was working for an oil company.

With therapy and medication, Amy managed to overcome her depression. She eventually completed her degree through another university that was closer to home.

After what happened to her, she decided she wanted to help other women who had suffered similar trauma. She tried to bring charges against Kyle, but no lawyer would touch her case. The event had happened a long time ago. In some states, the statute to press charges had expired. Plus, her memory of the night was questionable.

Amy soon gave up her pursuit of justice and moved on with her life.

She was now in a stable relationship with a man who was kind, gentle, and decent. They were going to get married the following year. His work involved him being away for long stretches at a time, but they always managed to talk to each other every night.

Amy got out of bed and washed up. She went downstairs to the kitchen. Normally, her fiancé would have already placed the pot on to brew. The entire house would smell of coffee. She loved it.

He would also make her breakfast, which was something else she loved about him. That day, it was up to her to get everything ready. She grabbed the pot and put it on to brew.

She grabbed two eggs and some sausages from the fridge. She put them in a pan and began to fry them. She turned on the television and flipped the channel to the news.

While she made breakfast, she listened to what was happening in the city.

She had her meal and then put the dishes in the sink. She then stood by the back window, finishing her cup of coffee.

She noticed something odd. There was something hanging from the tree in the backyard.

She went outside to see what it was.

As she got closer, her jaw nearly dropped.

Hanging from a rope around his neck was the body of a man. Blood covered his entire body. His lifeless eyes were open, staring directly at her.

It did not take Amy long to realize the man was Kyle Summers.

Amy dropped her empty cup and ran inside.

## TWENTY-FIVE

Tarik parked his Mercedes next to a fire hydrant. Irina, who was sitting next to him, asked, "Should you be parking here?"

"Look around you. Where should I park?"

The street was choked with over a dozen vehicles. Some were law enforcement, but most were from the media.

Tarik said, "I don't know how these guys find out so quickly."

"I bet the 9-1-1 dispatcher must have tipped them off."

Tarik thought for a moment. "Or maybe someone in the media is listening in on 9-1-1 calls."

"Would not surprise me," Irina said.

They got out.

As they walked up to the house, Tarik looked around at the parked vehicles. He did not see Jo's Jetta. Normally, she would be the first one on the scene.

They showed their credentials to the officer stationed outside the house. They moved to the front door and found Walters waiting for them in the hallway.

"We came as fast as we could," Tarik said.

"Good. We've got a dead body in the backyard."

They moved through the house. They saw a woman in the kitchen. She had her head in her hands and looked visibly shaken.

The FBI had erected tarps around the backyard as temporary walls to shield the crime scene from prying eyes.

Tarik at first did not understand why the walls were so high until he saw the victim hanging from the tree. "Another one?" he asked.

"We can't be sure," Walters replied.

"We can," said a voice from behind them. It was Ben Nakamura. Unlike the other day, Ben's attire was subdued. Instead of bright colors, he was dressed mostly in black and gray.

"What do you mean?" Walters asked.

"Even though I haven't examined the body up close yet, I can tell just by looking that the victim's blood was drained prior to him dying."

"How can you be so sure?" Irina asked.

"The discoloration of the skin," Ben replied. "And it was most likely done with a sharp blade across the neck. Same method used on the previous victim."

Walters frowned. "So, we have a serial killer on our hands."

"We should call Jo," Tarik said. "Did someone notify her?"

"Jo's not coming," Walters replied.

"Why not?" Tarik, Irina, and Ben asked in unison.

"She's on vacation."

Tarik laughed. "Yeah, right. Jo wouldn't miss this for anything. We better call her, or else she will be super pissed for missing this one."

"No," Walters said. "We're doing this without her."

Walters glanced over at Ben. She could tell he was somewhat relieved she was not there.

Walters said, "Tarik, you have seniority. You're in charge of this investigation."

Tarik felt unsure, but he said, "Yes, ma'am."

He walked over to the tree and looked up. There was a sign around the victim's neck.

"*I'm a rapist?*" Tarik said, reading the words aloud.

Ben came over. "I think I know the case. I was a student at a university not too far from the one where it happened. The victim's name is Kyle Summers."

Tarik made a face. "The name sounds familiar. Wasn't he ranked one of the top ten college football players in the country?"

"That's the one," Ben said. "We heard rumors he'd done something really bad, but we just never knew what it was. Until now, I guess."

"The woman inside… was she the victim?" Tarik asked.

Ben shrugged. "Could be, but like I said, it was only a rumor, and we didn't actually know what Kyle Summers had done wrong."

"It would explain why his body is in her backyard," Tarik said.

Irina joined them. "Do you think she did it?"

Tarik said, "I doubt that. You saw her. She's half his size and probably half his weight. I can't see her lifting his body up and hanging it on the tree."

"If someone ever took advantage of me like this jerk," Irina said, "I'd castrate him with a butcher knife."

Ben made a face. "That's good to know, I guess."

"Plus," Tarik said, keeping the conversation on track, "why would she kill the man who assaulted her years ago and then display his body on her property? She'd be incriminating herself in his murder. If this is related to the body at the hardware store, then we know it's a *man* who is behind this."

They stared at Summers's lifeless body.

"Do you mind if I bring him down?" Ben asked. "I can't perform an examination in the air."

"Oh, yeah, sure," Tarik replied.

A ladder was brought over, and two officers went up and pulled the body down.

Walters said to Tarik and Irina, "Find this killer fast before he kills a third time."

## TWENTY-SIX

Tarik and Irina spent the better part of the morning canvassing the neighborhood. They spoke to anyone who might have seen or heard anything the night before. Most of the neighbors had no idea something had happened, but they all had nothing but good words for Amy Lange. She was kind, sweet, and a wonderful neighbor. If there was a death in someone's family, Amy would be the first to reach out and offer her sympathy and support. She would invite kids from her street over to her house for parties. She would drive her elderly neighbors to their appointments and back. And if an abused woman needed a place to stay for a few nights, Amy was more than willing to offer her home.

Tarik and Irina got the idea that the neighbors were doing everything to make sure the authorities did not think Amy was a suspect. They repeatedly made it clear she was not, but it seemed like her neighbors did not believe them, and why would they? For example, the neighbor on her left, a man who worked as an engineer, had a clear view of the backyard, and he had seen the body the moment the police had arrived at Amy's house. He knew how serious the situation was. But there was another neighbor, a man who worked in computer programming, who thought Amy may have committed the crime. "Maybe she snapped, drove all the way to Texas, brought him back to town, killed him, and put him on display," he suggested to Tarik and Irina.

Tarik and Irina glanced at each other. "Thank you for your time, sir," Tarik said as he and Irina stood to leave. He could tell Irina thought the same as he did: the man was being sensationalistic.

The neighbor behind Amy's house, a woman who was a retired school teacher, had something interesting to tell them. "Last night, I heard a car pull up to the road next to my house," she said. "I was in bed, so I didn't get up to check. I felt there was no reason for concern. Cars stop there all the time."

"What happened next?" Tarik asked.

"I heard the car door open and shut, and then the trunk. I thought somebody was being dropped off, but I did not hear anyone say 'thank you' or 'goodbye.' I thought that was strange."

"Did you hear anything else?" Irina asked her.

"Yes. I heard what sounded like someone was dragging a heavy bag past my home."

"Did you see who was making the noise?" Tarik asked.

The woman shook her head. "I had already taken my Melatonin, and I was falling asleep fast. I did not know what I heard might have had something to do with a murder until I found out what had happened."

Tarik thanked the woman, then he and Irina walked through the woman's side yard. They saw marks on the dirt path. If they had to take a guess, they were made by the victim's heels as he was dragged along.

The neighbor's backyard was attached to Amy's backyard. "Why didn't the killer just drag Summers through Amy's side yard?" Irina asked Tarik.

The answer came when they saw the height of the fence between the two houses. It was barely six feet. It would not have taken the killer a great deal of trouble to heave the body over the fence and then cross it himself. There was also a problem with going through Amy's side yard. The gate leading to the backyard was eight feet high and the top was curved. Climbing the gate would require a lot of effort, much less heaving a body over it.

The best way into Amy's backyard was through the neighbor's side of the house. Tarik and Irina quickly deduced that the killer had surveyed Amy's property and the surrounding area in advance.

There was something else Tarik and Irina had noticed when they had gone door to door. None of the neighbors had security cameras on their premises. But even if they did, the killer probably would have disguised himself like he did at the hardware store.

Whoever was behind this was willing to go through great lengths to make a statement. Tarik and Irina wished they knew what that statement was.

## TWENTY-SEVEN

Rhodes was sitting outside his apartment when he saw the Cadillac drive up to the house. Yevgeny got out. The moment Yevgeny saw Rhodes, his face contorted into a grimace. "I knew I recognized you from somewhere," he said, walking up to Rhodes. "Why did you drive up to me and say my name? And what were you doing there?"

"I was following you," Rhodes said.

Yevgeny looked confused. "Why would you do that?"

"I wanted to see what you were up to," Rhodes said in a matter-of-fact tone. "I saw how you and your boys spotted the vehicles you were planning to steal."

Yevgeny's face turned menacing. "Are you for real, man?"

"I am, and I know what goes on in that garage."

Yevgeny crossed his arms over his chest. "Tell me. What goes on in there?"

"Stolen vehicles are brought in to be taken apart and sold in pieces on the black market."

Yevgeny laughed. "What're you, a cop?"

"I used to be."

Yevgeny's smile faded.

"My name is Martin Rhodes. I used to be a homicide detective."

Yevgeny stared at him for a good minute. "If you are who you say you are, then what the hell are you doing in my mom's basement? It's a shit hole. Can't you see that?"

"It is, but I've got no place else to go."

"Why not?"

"I shot and killed a man. I served ten years in prison for it."

Yevgeny's mouth nearly dropped. Someone like him was a small-time crook. They committed crimes that were mostly misdemeanors. They never graduated to big-time crimes because they were too weak or afraid to pull the trigger.

Rhodes had seen too many posers in his years. They spent most of their free time watching gangster movies. They thought this made them tough as if they were somehow part of the streets. While Yevgeny's father may have been a thug in Russia, Yevgeny had been shielded somewhat in America by his mother. He may have wished to be like his father, but he was nowhere close to being like him. Rhodes had come across a lot of young men inside and outside prison who acted like punks. He could tell the wannabes from the real deal.

Yevgeny quickly composed himself. He said with a grin, "I've been to prison. It was no big deal."

Rhodes could easily tell Yevgeny was boasting, trying to impress him. "You were probably kept with the general population where you were allowed to exercise, have a meal with other inmates, go to the library... hell, even join a prison club. But people like me, those who committed violent crimes and have no chance of seeing the outside for a very long time, are kept locked up twenty-three hours a day. When you spend that long staring at a wall, you can't wait to unleash whatever rage that has festered inside you on another human being."

Yevgeny swallowed. His forehead beaded with sweat. "Why are you telling me all this?"

"I don't want you to end up back in prison, that's why."

"Why do you care what happens to me?"

"Your mom asked me to talk to you."

Yevgeny smiled again. "First of all, it's none of your business what I do, and second of all, I won't be going back."

"You're stealing cars again, Yevgeny."

"You got no proof of that."

"The police are watching the auto garage."

Yevgeny smirked. "We know about that. It's not hard to spot them. But the cops got nothing on us."

"They know about the other chop shops." This was a lie, but Yevgeny did not know if Rhodes was telling the truth or not. "And very soon, they will raid them, and when they do, you'll be in more trouble than you care to be in."

Yevgeny scowled. "I'll tell my buddies what you just told me."

Rhodes shook his head. "I wouldn't do that if I were you."

"And why not?"

"They'll ask how you found out. You want to tell them you talked to an ex-cop? Heck, they probably already think you and I know each other."

Yevgeny turned pale. "That's why you drove up and called out my name outside the garage."

"When the police raid your buddies' garage, I'll spread the rumor that you talked to the police. When the news spreads to the prisons, don't be surprised if someone shanks you. No one likes a rat."

Yevgeny was almost in tears. "But I would never talk to the police."

"They don't know that," Rhodes said.

"I never gave anyone up before, and I would never give anyone up now."

"The last time was different. I wasn't involved then. Now I am. And believe me, I will make sure everyone knows how you helped the police."

"But I didn't," Yevgeny protested.

"It doesn't matter. What matters is that you get yourself out before the hammer comes down. You were just released from prison. They won't suspect you. Tell them you need to take care of your mother. She's sick. But if you stick around long enough for the police to swoop in, then they'll know something was up. The last thing you want is to be back in prison with a reputation as a police snitch."

Yevgeny's hands began to tremble.

Rhodes opened his car door. "Think about it, but don't think too long. Time is running out."

He got in and drove off.

## TWENTY-EIGHT

Rhodes decided to go straight to a bar. He had had a busy day and needed some alcohol in his system to calm him down.

He was not sure that what he told Yevgeny would change his mind. It was not like he expected a light bulb to flash on in the kid's head and he would suddenly go down the right path. No. Things normally did not work that way. People did wake up and decide to alter their lives, but that was because they had experienced an event that was a catalyst for change. Up until Rhodes confronted Yevgeny, he had likely never second-guessed his involvement in stealing cars. He probably figured it was the best decision he had ever made. He got to hang out with his buddies and make some easy cash on the side. So what if he got caught? He would do some time and be out before he knew it. It was a life he was familiar with, given his family's history.

*It must not have been easy seeing your father in prison*, Rhodes thought. This was something Rhodes could relate to. Whenever his old man was locked up, it felt like the entire town knew. Kids at school would tease Rhodes, and even his teachers would ask what his father had done this time. At first, he thought it was the police who were picking on his father. After all, no child ever saw their parents as the bad guys. It was only when he grew up that he realized his old man could not help himself from getting into trouble. He had been in and out of prison so many times that whenever the cops showed up, they let him get dressed, sometimes have a meal, and even say goodbye to his family. They probably felt sorry for him. He knew no other life than the one he had been raised in.

Rhodes used to miss his father very much when he was gone. He would constantly ask his mother, "When is dad coming back?" But when he started to understand his father's behavior, he started to wish for the police to come and take him away. His mother would cry each time they did, but she cried even more when he was around. At least when he was away, she could focus on Rhodes and herself. She did not have a drunk, hot-headed gambler of a husband to be concerned about.

Rhodes walked up to the bartender and ordered a glass of bourbon. When it came, he took the glass and found a booth in the corner.

He had taken a couple of sips when a Hispanic man walked into the bar. The man's head was shaved. He had a goatee, and he was wearing a loose, checkered shirt and baggy pants. He scanned the bar, spotted Rhodes, and walked over. Without saying a word, he slid into the seat across from him.

"I think you are at the wrong table," Rhodes said.

"I think I'm at the right table," the man replied. On his neck, just above his shirt collar, Rhodes could see tattoos. Even his knuckles had markings.

"I don't know you," Rhodes said.

"But I know you, Detective Martin Rhodes."

Rhodes's back stiffened.

"Actually, it's my cousin who knows you. Jesus Vasquez."

Rhodes tightened his grip on his glass.

Jesus was the leader of a Latino gang out on the West Coast. He was involved in everything: extortion, drugs, prostitution, and even murder. Jesus's reign of terror finally ended when he was caught on camera, conspiring to kill a judge. He was sentenced to ten years, but this turned into life when he was embroiled in a fight with two other inmates. One of those inmates was Rhodes. The other was a member of a rival gang.

Jesus despised the law and especially those who enforced it, which was why he wanted to go after the judge who had repeatedly sent him to prison. Jesus had a feeling the judge had targeted him and sooner or later would find something big to use against him. Jesus wanted to prevent that. He did not realize that word had gotten out about what he was up to, and the police had set a trap, which eventually led to his arrest and conviction.

When Jesus found out a former police detective was serving time in the same block as him, he smelled blood. He wanted to get revenge for all the times the police had wronged him, and he would make Rhodes an example.

What Jesus did not count on happening was that a rival street gang wanted him eliminated as well. With him locked up, they were already encroaching on his territory, and they did not want him coming out of prison and seeking retribution. Better to get rid of him now than have a bloodbath once he was freed.

On the day Jesus attacked Rhodes, the rival gang member took the opportunity to go after him too. The result was a fight so brutal that Rhodes was left with cuts on his arms, chest, and torso. Jesus was left with a broken nose, busted lip, and a welt on his head. The rival gang member was left in a far worse condition. He died from a stab wound to the heart, compliments of Jesus.

Witnesses at the scene stated it was Jesus who had picked the fight with Rhodes and that Rhodes was just trying to defend himself. Nonetheless, Rhodes got two weeks in the hole for his involvement. Jesus, on the other hand, got his sentence extended to life for killing another inmate.

Rhodes never imagined he would hear of Jesus Vasquez again.

"Your face tells me you remember my cousin," the man said with a smile.

"What's your name?" Rhodes asked.

"Paco."

"What do you want, Paco?"

"I could say I want revenge for what happened to my cousin, but I won't."

Rhodes's eyes narrowed. "Then what is it you want?"

Paco's smile widened. "I want money."

Rhodes was confused.

Paco leaned over and said, "Listen. I can't change what happened to my cousin. It's not like he's ever going to get out. But there are guys in his gang who will come after you if they found out where you are. You know what I'm saying?"

Rhodes understood. Paco would keep his mouth shut if Rhodes paid him. If he did not, he would inform Jesus's gang of his whereabouts, causing a big problem for Rhodes.

"How much?" Rhodes asked.

Paco shrugged. "I don't know. Let's say fifty grand."

"I don't have that kind of money," Rhodes said. "You do understand they don't give steady jobs to ex-convicts like us."

Paco nodded as if he had been through that himself. "Okay, twenty-five grand, and not a penny lower."

Rhodes was silent a moment. "How can I trust you?" he asked. "How do I know you won't tell Jesus's gang even after I give you the money?"

"Listen, bro, I don't want anyone to find out what I just told you, you get me?"

Rhodes nodded. Paco did not want Jesus's gang to know he was keeping silent in exchange for money. Jesus would have him killed if he found out.

Paco said, "But if you don't have the money, then I promise you, you are a dead man, got it?"

"I do."

"Good," Paco said as if he was proud of himself.

"How did you find me?" Rhodes asked.

"I was at the auto garage when you drove past it. You were loud when you called out that kid's name." Rhodes knew he was referring to Yevgeny. "It got everyone's attention, mine included. It was not very smart, what you did at the garage. If you hadn't done it, I wouldn't have known you were in Bridgeton."

Paco got up. "Enjoy your drink."

Rhodes watched as he left the bar.

Rhodes gritted his teeth. In his attempt to help Yevgeny, he had just brought a whole lot of trouble his way.

## TWENTY-NINE

The gun recoiled as the bullet was fired and hit the target.

Jo was at a shooting range. She had been there for over an hour.

The target was a hundred feet away, and Jo had hit it with almost every shot.

She reloaded and fired again.

She could not sit at home. Even after doing all the organizing and cleaning, she could not wait to get out. It was probably the longest time she had ever spent at home in years. Once, she had been hit with a severe viral infection, and doctors had ordered her on complete bed rest. After one day, she could not take the tedium anymore. She got in her car and drove to the office. She did not go in. Instead, she sat in the parking lot and watched officers and agents go in and out of the building.

Work had always been her solace. Even when she was feeling down, she could always rely on work to lift her spirits.

She knew this was not a healthy lifestyle. People spent time away from work in order to recuperate. She did the opposite.

It was always comforting knowing there was a mystery or puzzle to solve. Maybe it kept her mind away from the real problem: her heart.

She feared if she stopped and smelled the roses, so to speak, she would be reminded of what awaited her. The operation, the rehabilitation, and not to mention the time spent confined in bed.

That, above everything else, would be pure torture.

She could not imagine watching TV all day. What would she watch anyway? Soap operas? Trashy shows? Reruns of old sitcoms?

No. She could not imagine passing the time like that.

Maybe she could read a book? She could not remember the last one she had read from cover to cover. Fictional stories did not interest her. Real-life was more interesting.

Her job gave her excitement. It was not every day someone came face-to-face with a serial killer. When she was on a case, she felt alive, as if nothing else mattered—not even her health. Her only focus was on finding the person responsible for the evil crime.

At the moment, though, she did not even have that. By taking time off, she did not know what was happening to the case she had been working on.

She had thought about calling Tarik, Irina, or even Chris. But she did not know what she would tell them once they asked why she was away. She would have to give them an answer once she returned. She still had a few days to come up with something.

A man walked up to her. He was tall, and he had broad shoulders and a chiseled chin. He wore a tight t-shirt that exposed his chest and arms.

He smiled and said, "Nice shot."

"Thanks," Jo replied.

"If you ever want to shoot some real weapons, I know just the place," the man said. "M16s, Uzis, sniper rifles, even grenade launchers."

He was grinning from ear to ear.

"Why would I want to shoot a grenade launcher?" Jo asked, irritated.

"For fun, that's why."

"Unless some foreign force is invading my country, I don't really see the point of blowing stuff up. In fact, it's reckless and dangerous. You're better off playing video games. This way, you can act out your adolescent behavior without hurting anyone."

Before he could say something, she walked away.

## THIRTY

Rhodes was in his basement apartment when he heard pounding on the door. He stiffened. He was not expecting anyone. Tess had a key, so it could not be her.

Could it be Yevgeny? Maybe he decided he did not want Rhodes's advice after all. Maybe he brought his buddies to teach Rhodes a lesson for trying to interfere.

Could it be Paco? Maybe he decided he wanted the money right then. Or maybe he had changed his mind and did not want the money, wanting instead to put a bullet in Rhodes's head for what happened to his cousin.

It was moments like this when Rhodes wished he had a gun. He walked up to the door but did not stand in front of it. If someone had a high-powered weapon, it would be easy to fire a few rounds and hit Rhodes through the door.

"Who is it?" Rhodes asked.

"It's me… Sully," his father replied.

Rhodes's shoulders relaxed. He opened the door and found Sully standing at the entrance. "I've been knocking for ages, boy," he said.

"What're you doing here?" Rhodes asked.

"I came to give you this." Sully held up a business suit for him. It was light blue with black stripes, and there was a matching tie on the hanger the suit dangled from.

"What for?" Rhodes asked.

"It's for you to wear to my wedding." Before Rhodes could say something, Sully said, "I know you didn't give me an answer about being my best man, but Marty, I would really like you standing next to me."

"I don't think it's a good idea," Rhodes said.

"Come on, son. If it wasn't important to me, I wouldn't be asking you."

Rhodes realized the more he turned Sully down, the more Sully would try to convince him. Rhodes had too much on his plate already, and he did not need Sully to complicate his life even more. If all he had to do to get Sully off his back was show up to his wedding for an hour and then leave, Rhodes would do it.

Rhodes grabbed the suit. It looked tacky and needed a good dry cleaning.

"It's one of my old ones," Sully said. "I figured you and I are the same size now, so it should fit you."

"All right," Rhodes said. "I'll try it on."

Rhodes was about to close the door when Sully said, "You're not going to invite me in for a beer? I took a bus all the way here."

When Rhodes was younger, he had lost count of the times Sully would drop him off at a friend's house, a school event, or even something Sully wanted him to do, and would then forget to pick him up. Rhodes would have to ask his friend's parents to give him a ride, or a teacher to give him money for a bus ticket, or even walk an hour just to get home. And when he would ask Sully about it, instead of apologizing for being negligent, Sully would blast him for even bringing the topic up. "Don't you realize I am a busy man?" Sully would rant. "You should be thankful for getting a ride, Martin. I'm not your chauffeur." But his bluster was his way of covering up for doing stuff that was more important to him than being a father. Rhodes knew that stuff involved drinking at a bar, gambling at a casino, or wasting time with his buddies at some club. Setting priorities was not something Sully spent too much time thinking about.

Rhodes said, "I'll see you at the wedding, Sully."

He shut the door on him.

# THIRTY-ONE

Chris bit down on his fingernail until he realized he had bitten too far. Whenever he was nervous or anxious, he would revert to his childhood habit of biting his nails.

He felt like he was going to have a nervous breakdown. Ever since Irina agreed to go out with him, he could not function properly. All he could think about was the big night.

He never thought it would happen. She was way out of his league. If she was a ten, he was a minus-twenty when it came to being hot.

*What was I thinking when I kept asking her out?* he thought. *Surely, in her right mind, she would never say yes.*

Maybe that was why he was persistent. He knew there was not even a remote possibility of that happening, so why not keep trying? It was actually fun. He enjoyed seeing her repulsed at the thought of being on a date with him. It was not like he did not fancy her. Who wouldn't? She was tough, independent, and—in case he forgot to mention it—*hot*.

He was more interested in the chase. Like the ones in the cartoons where Wile E. Coyote was never able to catch the Road Runner. And now that he had finally gotten the chance to be with her on one date, he feared he would somehow mess up and she would forever hold that against him.

He needed something to calm his nerves. He was not a drinker or a smoker. He had tried playing video games, but even those did not help. That was when he knew he was in way over his head.

He got up and went to the bathroom. He splashed cold water on his face. He should call it off. He should tell Irina it was a mistake. Guys like him did not have a chance with girls like her. Their night would end up being a joke. Plus, she was only doing it to get him off her back. She was not interested, to begin with. Why go through with the date then? It was better to save both of them the misery.

He would tell her the date was canceled.

He left the bathroom and headed for her desk. It was empty, but in the breakroom, he spotted Tarik.

He quickly went over to him.

"Hey, Tarik," he said, rubbing his hands.

"Hey, Chris," he replied. Tarik was pouring himself a cup of coffee.

"Can I talk to you?"

"Sure. What's up?"

"Um, I was… um… thinking of canceling my date with Irina."

Tarik frowned. "Why would you do that?"

"You know why. She's only doing it because I kept pushing her to."

Tarik took a sip from his cup. "So what? Don't you want to go out on a date with her?"

"I do, but now I'm thinking it might be a bad idea."

Tarik gave Chris a wry look. "Listen, I warned you to be careful with what you wished for."

"I know. It ended up happening, and now I'm freaked out."

"And you want to back out?"

"Yeah, but I don't know how to do it."

Tarik leaned over and said, "Let me tell you something about women. You cannot stand them up. If they turn you down, that's okay, but don't think they won't take it personally if you did it."

"But Irina never wanted to go out with me in the first place. She'd be happy if we canceled the date."

"That's where you're wrong. Even if she didn't want to go, there is no way she would accept that it was *you* who stood her up. In fact, she'd take it very personally. She might even think you were playing a prank when you asked her out in front of the team only to turn her down after she finally accepted."

"Then what do I do?" Chris asked.

"Go through with it."

Chris swallowed. He pushed his hand through his hair. "So, where do I take her out?"

"How would I know?" Tarik said.

"You must know something. You work with her."

"Yeah, exactly. I work with her. I'm not friends with her."

Chris fell silent.

Tarik broke into a smile. "I'm just messing with you, man," he said. "Irina acts all tough and rough. You would think she'd be happy to go to a bar and watch a football game, but what she really wants is a guy to treat her like a queen."

Chris rubbed his chin. "A queen, huh?"

"Yeah, show up at her house in a tuxedo and bring her flowers. And then take her to a fancy restaurant."

"Are we talking expensive? Because my bank account—"

"Do you want to impress her or not?" Tarik asked.

"I do."

"Then at the fancy restaurant, you order their special bottle of wine."

"What about food?"

"Don't cheap out. In fact, you order for her. She likes a man who takes charge."

"Are you sure?"

Tarik frowned. "If you don't believe me, why are you asking me?"

"No, no, no." Chris put his hands up. "I believe you."

"Make sure she feels like she is taken care of. Got it?"

Chris nodded. "I think so."

## THIRTY-TWO

Rhodes was at a diner. He already had consumed a muffin, a croissant, two cups of coffee, and was now working through his third cup.

He checked his watch and frowned. He was about to get up and walk over to the pay phone in the corner when he spotted Tess enter through the front door.

She looked around, saw him, and came over.

"Sorry I'm late," she said, dropping her backpack on the seat next to her.

"I was about to call you," Rhodes said. "Is everything okay?"

"Yeah, why wouldn't it be?"

"I mean, I haven't seen you around the house."

"I've been busy, you know."

"I even knocked on your door. Your mom wasn't too happy to see me, but she said you were out."

"I was."

"Doing what?"

She gave him a look. "Are you interrogating me?"

"No, I'm just concerned."

"Don't be. I'm fine," she said, shoving her hand in her backpack. She pulled out her laptop. "I did answer my cell phone when you called earlier, didn't I?"

Rhodes nodded. When he had not seen her for some time, he became worried. He thought something bad must have happened to her, but when he saw that her mom did not seem too concerned, he knew that was not the case. He also wanted to know how far Tess had gotten with the task he had given her.

She turned the laptop on and said, "I went through the security footage, and I think I saw something interesting."

"What?" Rhodes asked, sitting up in his chair.

"Did you order?" she asked, looking over at his cup. "I'm hungry."

*Kids and their appetites,* he thought. He waved the waiter over and ordered a hot chocolate, an egg salad sandwich, and a piece of chocolate cake. Rhodes knew he would be paying for Tess's food, but he did not care.

She turned the laptop so that he could get a better view and clicked the *play* button.

The security camera was facing the entrance of the venue where the rock concert was playing the night of the Goldsmith murders.

Tess said, "The concert was over two hours long, but people started lining up half an hour before that, so there were several hours of footage I had to go through." She fast-forwarded the video and stopped when the gates opened.

She and Rhodes watched as concertgoers passed through turnstiles. Once their tickets were scanned, they moved through security, where a guard checked their bags and scanned their bodies with a magnetic wand. The process was fast and effortless.

Dozens of concertgoers moved through the gates in a matter of minutes. They watched the line of people for several minutes until Tess said, "Look there." She pointed to a man in a t-shirt and jeans. The man had a buzz-cut hairstyle, and he was clean-shaven. He was also smiling from ear to ear.

Rhodes knew it was Adam Channing.

Behind Adam was another man, obviously his friend. He was dressed in a t-shirt and cargo pants, and he had a goatee. He was constantly laughing with Adam. They both looked excited to be at the concert.

Adam was carrying a backpack, which he obediently opened for the security guard to examine. When he and his friend had disappeared from view, Rhodes said, "Play it again."

They watched as Adam moved through the turnstile. "Stop it right there," Rhodes ordered.

Tess did.

Adam was looking up as if he was staring directly at the security camera.

"Run it," Rhodes said.

Adam then moved to the ticket collector, scanning the tickets. Adam looked up once again at the security camera. Rhodes knew he had caught Adam's look the first time he had seen it.

Adam then approached the security guard, and without being prompted, he quickly opened his backpack for him. He said something to the guard with a laugh, but the guard did not laugh back.

Adam looked up at the camera again.

*It was as if he wanted to be seen*, Rhodes thought.

When Adam and his friend left the screen, Rhodes leaned back. He was not sure what he had just seen. There was something odd about it, but then there was also something quite normal about Adam's behavior. Why was Adam so concerned about the camera that he kept turning to it? Maybe he was just so excited to be there that his focus kept diverting to it. That did not make him guilty, did it?

Rhodes shook his head and turned to Tess. Her order had come, and she had already dived in. "You said you saw something interesting. What was it?" Rhodes asked.

"Oh yeah," she said as if it had slipped her mind. She sped up the image. The concertgoers were gone, and the gates were empty. Almost twenty minutes of footage went by before she played it at normal speed.

"What're we watching?" Rhodes asked. There was nothing of interest. The only people he saw were the security guards and the ticket collector.

"Just wait," she said through a mouthful of sandwich.

A man appeared on the screen. His back was to the camera, but he was wearing a baseball cap and a light jacket. The man quickly moved past the turnstile and left the venue.

"What's so important about him?" Rhodes asked, confused.

"You'll see." She fast-forwarded the video again. While the image moved at lightning speed, she kept her focus on her sandwich. Almost an hour went by on the recording before she slowed to normal speed again.

"Keep watching," she said.

The man in the baseball cap and jacket returned. He showed his ticket to the ticket collector. They exchanged a few words, and after the security guard scanned him, he entered the venue. Never once did the man look up at the camera.

"What was so interesting about him?" Rhodes asked.

"Why leave after the concert has started and then return when it is almost at the end?" Tess replied.

"Maybe something came up and he had to run out," Rhodes said.

She shrugged. "Maybe. I just thought it was odd."

She fast-forwarded the video to the end. The gates opened again as people streamed out from the venue. Tess pressed *play* again and pointed to the monitor.

On the screen, Adam and his friend were walking past the security guard. Adam was waving his arms in circles and shouting. A guard warned him to take it outside, and Adam got into a heated argument with him. His friend intervened and dragged him out.

As he did so, Adam was looking directly at the camera again.

*He might have been securing evidence for his alibi*, Rhodes thought.

## THIRTY-THREE

Jo took a stroll in the park. She hoped a walk would help her relax. The time spent at the shooting range had calmed her, but when her visit was over, she was anxious once again.

She wished she could go and meet Dr. Cohen. She would tell him his advice was backfiring. Instead of feeling better, she was feeling worse. Her work was a distraction from her problems, and with no work to do, all she could do was think about what was wrong in her life.

She was not married, and she had no children. This was something she never cared for before, but after she met Mathias, she began to have a feeling that there was something missing in her life. Maybe it was her biological clock reminding her that time was running out.

But Jo never imagined herself as a mother. It was not something she aspired to be. Her decision may have seemed odd to her family and friends, but to her, it felt normal. Her mother had shown very little affection toward her and her brother. It wasn't that she did not care for her children. She did. It was just that she never went out of her way to hug them, kiss them, and tell them she loved them. It was her father who did that.

Maybe that was why her brother had paternal instincts, whereas she had no maternal instincts. He would be up late at night soothing Chrissy when she was a baby. He would take turns changing diapers. He would even give Chrissy a bath when Kim was at work. He was fully devoted to being a parent and was good at it.

Something occurred to Jo. She checked her watch and realized if she hurried, she could still meet him. She pulled out her cell phone and dialed a number.

Half an hour later, she was sitting by the window in a coffee shop across from a government building. She watched as Sam came out from the front entrance, checked the traffic on the road, and then came into the coffee shop. He was tall, thin, and he wore wire-rimmed glasses. His head was shaved ever since he started losing his hair in his twenties.

He spotted her and came over.

"So, what's this about, Jo?" he asked, grabbing a chair opposite her.

"I'm on vacation."

"So you told me. I don't believe you."

"It's only for a few days, but Dr. Cohen thinks it'll be good for my heart."

"And is it?"

She made a face. "You know me. I can't stay in one place long enough to get any rest."

"I thought so."

"Do you want anything? Coffee? Tea?"

He shook his head. "I've already had my break. My supervisor is not in today, so no one will know that I'm on my second break. When was the last time you dropped by my workplace?"

"I think… *never*," Jo replied.

"That's what I thought too. So are you here because you're bored?"

"Yes, and I wanted to talk to you."

"About what?"

Jo gave Sam a firm look. "I spoke to Kim. She told me you guys were going through a rough patch."

Sam looked away.

"She said you guys were thinking of separating."

Sam just stared out the window.

Jo leaned over and put her hand over his. "What's going on, Sam? You can talk to me."

"It's more complicated than that," he finally said.

"How? You and Kim are happy together, and with Chrissy, you are a perfect family."

"I know. It's just…"

He paused.

"What, Sam? Tell me."

He sighed. "Kim caught me texting someone."

"Who?"

"She works in another department in our building."

Jo's brow furrowed. "Are you having an affair?"

"No, no, no," he quickly replied. "It's not like that."

"Then what is it?"

"It was just some harmless flirting. She's married, and I'm married. We were never going to do anything."

Jo sighed. "Kim said you were spending too much time at work. Now I can tell why."

He shook his head. "I am busy at work. I've got a ton of cases on my desk. But I'm not having an affair, Jo."

"Why were you even flirting, Sam? If dad was here, he'd be disappointed in you."

"If dad was here, he wouldn't dare say anything to me," he replied with an edge in his voice.

"What's that supposed to mean?" Jo asked.

Sam waved his hand. "Forget I said anything."

"Sam, what are you talking about? Why wouldn't dad tell you what you did was wrong?"

"Because he did something far worse."

Jo froze. "What did you say?"

"Dad wasn't the saint you thought he was."

"Dad cheated on mom?" Jo asked.

Sam nodded. "Why do you think mom suddenly fell apart? It didn't happen after dad died. It happened before."

Jo felt her throat constrict. "Who was it?"

"It doesn't matter anymore. It was a long time ago."

"Sam." Jo's voice was hard. "You have no right to hide this from me. They are my parents too."

Sam looked at her. "You really want to know?"

"Yes."

"He had a fling with Charlotte Walters."

Jo's mouth dropped. "It's not possible…"

"It is," Sam said. "They were partners in the FBI, and they were having an affair. When mom found out, she went into a deep depression. They were going to split up, but dad ended up getting murdered."

"It's not true," Jo said. She felt numb.

"It is. Why do you think Walters wasn't at his funeral? Mom didn't want her there. The entire FBI was there, but she wasn't."

"She didn't come because she was too distraught. She told me so."

"What else was she going to say? She knows how much you adored dad."

Jo thought for a moment. "Why didn't you tell me?"

"I couldn't because I knew it would break your heart. Your heart is already too fragile. The last thing I wanted was for you to get hurt."

Jo stood up. Her eyes were filled with tears. "But I should've known, Sam. You should've told me."

She stormed out of the coffee shop.

# THIRTY-FOUR

It was a three-hour drive, but Tarik and Irina did not mind. The location they were going to investigate was better than going all the way to Texas, where Kyle Summers's driver's license was registered. Fortunately for them, Summers was receiving disability checks, which had given them a lead.

During their investigation, they discovered that Summers had last worked at a warehouse for a large furniture outlet, where he had re-injured the leg he had broken in college. However, there were three other instances where Summers had applied for disability benefits. And they were all in different states.

They had a feeling Summers was trying to scam the system.

They drove up to the building. Irina frowned. "It looks like a dump. Are you sure we're in the right place?"

Tarik checked his phone. "It's the address we have on file."

The walls of the building were covered in gang markings and other graffiti. The front door's glass was cracked. Two men were standing by the entrance, smoking what was clearly marijuana.

Irina looked around and said, "You sure it was a good idea to bring your Mercedes?"

Tarik's face did not betray him, but he was not sure either. "Come on, let's get this over with," he said.

They walked up to the entrance. The men by the door were dressed in baggy shirts, baggy jeans, and sneakers. One of them had on a bandana while the other sported cornrows.

They were eyeing the Mercedes, probably wondering what moron would bring a fancy car like that to such a run-down neighborhood.

As Tarik and Irina moved past them, Tarik made a dramatic show of adjusting his jacket, exposing the gun attached to his belt.

The eyes of one of the men widened. The other quickly hid the joint behind his back.

The building's main doors were not locked. Tarik and Irina were not surprised, considering the condition of the building was in.

They walked up to the elevators. Out of the three available, only one was working.

"You want to take the stairs?" Irina asked.

"It's on the seventh floor," Tarik replied.

"Come on, don't tell me you're scared of a little exercise," Irina teased.

"I was actually more concerned about you," he joked back.

In less than a minute, they were in the hallway on the seventh floor. Neither of them had broken a sweat.

There was yellow police tape across one of the doors, which told them it was the one they were looking for. Prior to coming over, they had contacted the local police and requested they secure the premises. The local police also provided them with a set of keys to the apartment, which Tarik and Irina had picked up on the way.

Tarik pulled out the keys. Irina said, "I doubt you're going to need them." She pointed to the door. It was slightly ajar.

They drew their weapons and went inside. What they found did not surprise them much. The entire place looked like it had been ransacked. There was no TV, sofa, or coffee table. The dust prints on the floors told them where the items used to sit. The kitchen was a mess. There were broken plates, glasses, and bowls on the floor. Dirty pots and pans were in the kitchen sink, and the microwave was missing. The bedroom was no better. The mattress was pushed to the side, and the clothes from the closet were scattered everywhere.

The bathroom was filthy, which told them Summers was not a clean and tidy person, to begin with. But they were certain he did not tear this place apart. Someone else did.

Whoever robbed the place was in a hurry, not caring about the police tape.

"I doubt we'll find anything useful here," Irina said. "The entire scene has been contaminated."

Tarik nodded.

They left the apartment and moved down the hall. They had reached the exit when a man stuck his head out from behind a door. His hair was thinning. His face was wrinkled, and he was in his pajamas. "You the cops?" he asked.

Tarik glanced over at Irina. "Yes, we are," he said to the man.

"Can I see your badges?" the man asked.

They flashed their credentials.

He smiled. He was missing several of his front teeth. "I had to be sure, you know," he said. "You guys here about the guy who got killed?"

"Yes," Tarik said. "Did you know him?"

The man shook his head. "I only said hi to him a few times. He wasn't very friendly. He kept to himself. We all do, really. You can't be sure who is living next to you. They could be pimps, drug dealers, even murderers, for all you know."

"How did you know he was killed?" Irina asked.

"I saw it on the news. I'm probably the only one in the building who's got a satellite dish. It's on the balcony, and I'm on the seventh floor, or else the people who live here would steal it in a heartbeat."

"Someone took the deceased's belongings. Do you know who that could be?" Irina asked.

"I wish I did, but I'm not surprised. People here will break down your door if they think you have something valuable at home. It's why I have several locks on my door."

"Did you see or hear anything that might help us find who killed your neighbor?" Tarik asked.

"No, not really, but I do remember something when I was coming back from church. I make sure to go a couple of times a week. On Tuesdays, they have pot roast, and my pension checks barely pay the rent, so it's nice to have a good meal every other day."

Tarik had a feeling the old man wanted to talk, but he did not want to rush him in case he knew something vital.

The man said, "It was late, and I was walking back home. I usually take a short cut and enter from the back of the building. That's when I saw it."

"Saw what?" Tarik and Irina asked in unison.

"A fancy car."

"What was special about it?" Tarik asked. He felt somewhat disappointed.

"Look around you," the man said. "In this neighborhood, did you see any fancy cars?"

Tarik thought about his Mercedes.

"We didn't look," Irina said.

"Well, when you drive back, see for yourself, and you'll realize most folks here can barely afford a car, let alone a fancy one."

"And this caught your eye?" Irina asked.

"Sure did. It was shiny and clean. I was worried someone would tear it apart."

"What did it look like?"

The man's brow furrowed. "What do you mean?"

"It's color?"

"Black, but it could've been gray. It was dark, you know."

"Model?"

"I never owned a car, so I wouldn't know."

"Did you get the license plate number by any chance?"

"I never thought to look. But the next morning when I went out for my walk, the car was no longer there."

They realized the old man was wasting their time.

"Thanks for letting us know," Tarik said as he moved toward the stairs.

"There was something else," the old man said.

"What?" Irina asked with a hint of annoyance.

"When I was walking down the hall to my apartment, I passed by the guy's door, and I heard something inside."

"What?" Tarik asked.

"It sounded like someone was crying."

"Crying?"

"Yeah, and I heard the guy say that he needed a doctor, or that he was the doctor, or that he knew a doctor. I couldn't tell for sure, but I could clearly tell the guy was distraught."

"And you didn't think to knock on his door or contact the police?" Irina asked.

He shrugged. "We have the police come here all the time. Plus, I thought maybe the guy was on drugs. You wouldn't believe the kind of crazy shit these guys do and say when they are high."

Tarik and Irina realized their lead was a dead end.

They took the stairs down. When they were outside, Tarik froze in front of his car. Someone had taken all four tires. They had placed concrete blocks underneath them in order to keep the vehicle above ground.

"I guess we're taking a taxi back to Bridgeton," Irina said.

Tarik put his face in his palms. *If there's a time to cry, this is it*, he thought.

# THIRTY-FIVE

Jo drove around the city, lost in a maelstrom of anger and confusion. She could not believe what Sam had told her.

She felt like she had been carrying a lie all her life. She always thought her parents had a perfect marriage that only ended because of her father's death.

When she was younger, there were many times when she would imagine what their lives would have been like if her father was still alive. She would imagine them going on picnics, going to the movies, and taking trips to Disneyland and other attractions.

She had become so obsessed with the man who had taken her father from her that she wanted to be an FBI agent just to catch him. The killer had destroyed the ideal life they were going to have. He had stripped them of all the joy they rightly deserved. And Jo was going to punish him for it.

What she did not know was that it did not matter what happened to her father because their family was already on the brink of collapse. It was not her father's death that had destroyed her mother; it was his betrayal. He had cheated on her, and with none other than—Jo's grip tightened on the steering wheel—*Charlotte Walters*.

She could not believe the woman who was like a second mother to her would do something like that. She could not believe Walters was the cause of all her mother's pain. Maybe that was why Walters was always good to Jo. Walters knew the damage she had done to Jo's family and was trying to make up for it. She was always concerned for Jo's well-being. So much that when Jo had approached her about joining the Bureau, she had tried to discourage her. She did not want anything to happen to Jo. It was bad enough that her father was gone. She could not bear seeing something bad happen to his daughter.

But Jo was persistent. There were two very good reasons she wanted to join the Bureau: She wanted to follow in her father's footsteps and become a federal agent, and she wanted to finish what her father had started and catch the Bridgeton Ripper.

Maybe if she had known about Walters and her father, she might not have been so keen on becoming an agent. She definitely would not have worked under Walters. How could she do that to her family? How could she destroy a marriage? How could she never mention to Jo what she did?

Jo exhaled. She realized Walters was not entirely to blame for what happened. Her father was just as complicit, maybe even more so. Jo had revered the man so much that she could not imagine him ever doing anything wrong. He was her hero, but he was also human. He had strengths, but he also had weaknesses.

There was more to him than what she chose to believe. Perhaps if he were still alive, she would not have idolized him. She might have seen him for who he was and not what she thought he was.

Jo had perceived her father incorrectly, but it was not her fault. The people who knew the truth had chosen to keep it hidden from her, leaving her to fantasize about a future that would never be if her father had lived. Her mother would have left her father, and Jo and Sam would have been shuttling back and forth between parents.

This reminded Jo of how vital a single piece of information was to an investigation. One piece of evidence had the power to turn a person from guilty to not guilty or vice versa.

If she knew the truth about her father sooner, perhaps her life would have turned out differently.

She drove on, struggling to calm herself.

## THIRTY-SIX

Rhodes was in a bar when Paco entered and headed straight for his booth.

He slid into the seat across from him, and his lips curled into a smile. "I thought you wouldn't show up."

"Why wouldn't I?" Rhodes asked.

Paco shrugged. "I don't know. You're an ex-con and I don't trust you. I was sure you'd skip town."

"I didn't."

"Do you have my money?" Paco asked.

"First, I want guarantees," Rhodes said.

"Like what?"

"I want you to guarantee that after I pay you, you won't run to Jesus's gang and tell them about me."

Paco made a face. "Why would I do that?"

"Jesus is your cousin. You must want revenge for what happened to him."

Paco laughed. "Jesus is a joke. He's a bully who thought he could push people around by scaring them. I wasn't scared of him. I was the only one who ever spoke up to him. The problem with him was he was a gangster, but I'm a businessman. With the money you're going to give me, I'll take over his gang. Once his boys see who's got the dollars, they'll forget about Jesus. He can rot in jail for all I care."

Paco crossed his arms over his chest and looked out the window. Rhodes could see tattoos underneath the sleeves. He could also see dark marks underneath the tattoos on his neck. They looked like someone had put a knife to his neck. The way Paco was ready to throw his cousin under the bus told Rhodes that Jesus was not very pleasant to him. He may have hurt him on numerous occasions to teach him a lesson. From what Rhodes knew about Jesus, he could be a homicidal maniac once he lost his temper. Rhodes would have felt sorry for Paco if he was not trying to extort money from him.

"So, where is the cash?" Paco asked.

"I don't have it."

Paco looked shocked and disappointed. "You sure about that?" he asked.

"I am."

"You know if you don't have the cash, I'll do what I have to do, right?"

"I understand," Rhodes answered.

Paco was confused. "Jesus's boys will kill you once I tell them where you are."

"We'll see about that."

A man stood up from the booth behind Rhodes's. The man was skinny as a twig. His neck and arms were covered in tattoos. He even had a teardrop tattooed under his right eye. When he opened his mouth, he revealed a golden canine tooth.

"What's up, Paco?" he said.

Paco suddenly turned pale. "Raul, what're you doing here?"

"I was gonna ask you the same thing," Raul said.

Two more men appeared, motioned for the bartender to take off, and surrounded the booth. One was almost six-five and over two hundred and eighty pounds. His head was shaved, but he had a large tattoo covering his skull. The second man was of medium height and medium build. His hair was gelled back, but instead of tattoos, his face was covered in piercings.

Paco looked at them both and swallowed. "It's not what you think," he said.

"Don't tell me what to think, Paco," Raul spat. "I heard everything. If this guy didn't call and tell me to come down here, I would have thought he was lying."

Paco pointed to Rhodes. "You can't trust him. He was trying to set me up, man."

"No, Paco. You were trying to set *us* up."

"He's a dirty cop," Paco said. "You can't believe anything he says."

"I don't believe him, but I know what you said about Jesus. And trust me, when I tell Jesus, he's not gonna be too happy."

The big guy moved toward Paco.

Paco put his hands up. "Listen, Raul. I was going to take the money from him and then I was going to share it with you guys, I swear, man. After that, I was also going to tell you where to find him."

"Shut up, Paco," Raul said.

The big guy grabbed Paco by his shirt collar and pulled him out of the booth.

Raul turned to Rhodes. "Thanks for calling us."

Rhodes nodded.

Raul pulled out a gun and pointed it at him. "Sorry, but I gotta do this. I gotta punish you for what you did to Jesus. If I don't, then Jesus will punish me. You understand me, right?"

Rhodes nodded. "I do."

"Get up. We're going for a ride."

They lead Paco and Rhodes into a waiting SUV.

Raul and the guy with the piercings got in the front while Paco, Rhodes, and the big guy got in the back. It was a little cramped, but neither Rhodes nor Paco complained with Raul pointing a gun at them.

Throughout the ride, Paco begged and pleaded with Raul. He told them they were making a big mistake. If Jesus found out they had a gun on him, he would have their heads.

Raul was having none of it. He was always suspicious of Paco. He knew one day he would betray the gang. He just did not think he would sell out his own cousin to an ex-cop. "That's worse than shooting Jesus in the head," he said to Paco.

"Please, man, let me go," Paco whined.

Rhodes kept his mouth shut. He knew whatever he had to say would do him no good. Raul would only become more irate, and Rhodes did not want an angry gangbanger getting an itchy trigger finger.

They drove for almost an hour until the SUV turned onto an empty street.

Rhodes looked out the window and saw only industrial buildings. They turned into a vacant parking lot and then came to a stop.

"Get out," Raul ordered them.

Paco and Rhodes did as instructed.

"Get down on your knees," Raul demanded.

Rhodes obliged, but Paco did not.

"Don't do this, Raul." Paco sounded defiant, but Rhodes could tell he was bluffing. "You don't know who you're messing with."

"I know exactly what I'm doing."

"When Jesus finds out, he'll—"

Raul finally smiled. "It was Jesus who ordered us to do this."

Paco's eyes widened.

Raul said, "Jesus wanted you gone for a long time. He just didn't know how to do it because you are his family. But now he can say he killed a traitor. Get down on your knees!"

"No," Paco spat. "I won't do it."

Raul cocked the gun and shot Paco in the thigh.

Paco collapsed to the ground, clutching his leg. "You shot me! You shot me!" he cried, all false bravado gone.

"You should've listened to me when I asked nicely," Raul said.

He turned to Rhodes. "Sorry, man, I know you made this happen, but it's nothing personal. Not for me, at least. You get me?"

"I understand. You have to do what you have to do."

Raul smiled. "I like you. I can see you can take it like a man."

Raul pointed his gun at Rhodes's head.

Sirens sounded. Before Raul and his boys knew what had happened, two unmarked police cars came screeching in, followed by several black-and-whites.

The cars encircled the group, and police officers leaped out, guns in hand. A man in a trench coat got out of one of the unmarked cars and said, "Put down your weapon or we'll shoot you dead."

Raul looked around. They were outnumbered.

He cursed and dropped the gun. He then got on his knees and put his hands in the air. Another man got out of the other unmarked car and came over to Rhodes. He was smiling from ear to hear. "We made it just in time," Mac said.

"One more minute, and you'd have been taking me to the morgue," Rhodes said.

The man in the trench coat approached them. "I'm Detective Hornsby. We've been following Jesus's gang for a while now. When Detective MacAfferty called us about your situation, we were more than happy to help out."

"For a moment there, I thought I was all by myself," Rhodes said.

"We were tracking you from the bar. We just wanted to catch them in action."

Rhodes nodded.

He watched as Raul and his boys were escorted into the squad cars. Paco was on the ground, still clutching his leg. One officer came over to administer first aid before the paramedics arrived. Once Paco's leg was treated, Rhodes knew he would be arrested for extortion and affiliation with a known criminal gang.

Mac turned to Rhodes, "Come. I'll give you a ride."

## THIRTY-SEVEN

As they drove, Mac said, "You find anything that might help with the Goldsmiths' case?"

"I've got some questions first," Rhodes said.

"Okay, shoot."

"Does Adam own a car?"

Mac shook his head. "He can't even afford a place of his own. That's why he's crashing at his friend's house."

"Does his friend own a car?"

Mac made a face. "I think it was a white Ford Taurus around ten years old."

"How far was the concert venue from the Goldsmiths' house?" Rhodes asked.

"I would say maybe less than half an hour."

Rhodes thought for a moment and said, "Can you find out if there are any convenience stores or gas stations around the Goldsmiths' house?"

"I can, but why?"

"Places like those are usually open late at night. If you find one, can you check their security footage?"

"Okay, but what will I be looking for?"

"Check to see if a vehicle matching the Ford Taurus drove by there."

Mac paused. "I've known you long enough to know you're working on an angle. Do you mind sharing it with me?"

"I'm not sure, but I have a feeling Adam was in two places at once."

Mac looked at him. "How is that possible?"

"It is when you are not looking carefully."

"Okay, so are you saying Adam was at the concert venue *and* at the Goldsmiths' house on that night?"

"Yes."

Mac's face twisted. "Unless he teleported, I'm not sure how he did it."

"I've seen the footage, and it confirmed what the security guards said. Adam and his friend arrived at the venue before the concert began. So, we have him entering the venue and leaving the venue, yes?"

"Yes."

"But what about in between?"

"What do you mean?"

"Could it be possible that Adam left during the concert, drove less than half an hour to the Goldsmiths' house, committed the murder, and then returned before the concert ended?"

"It's possible, but why didn't the security guards ever see him leave or enter while the concert was still in progress?"

"Maybe they weren't looking for him. Maybe he changed his attire, so he couldn't be recognized."

Mac's mouth dropped. "You saw him leave?"

"Not exactly, but I did see a man wearing a baseball cap and jacket leave the concert in the middle and return right before it ended. He never once looked up at the cameras, while Adam always did, as if he wanted to be seen."

"And you think it was Adam leaving in the middle of the concert?"

"I don't know. It could be anyone, but if you are certain Adam killed the Goldsmiths, then you have to consider the possibility."

Mac was dumbfounded. "I can't believe I didn't see it."

"Let's not jump to conclusions," Rhodes said. "It might be nothing, but I do feel it's worth looking into. Also, check who bought the concert tickets, and how many."

"How many?"

"Yes."

When Mac dropped Rhodes off at his apartment, he found Olya waiting for him by his front door.

Before Rhodes could say something, she came up and hugged him. "Thank you," she said.

Rhodes was taken aback. "What for?" he asked.

"My son did not go with his friends today," Olya replied. "He wants to work with his uncle in his plumbing business. Thank you so much, Mr. Rose."

"You're welcome," he said, moving toward the door. Rhodes was not comfortable with compliments. He always felt like he did not deserve them.

Whenever he solved a case and the grieving family tried to thank him, he wanted to get away as quickly as possible. He felt he was only doing his job. He did not need to be appreciated for it.

Olya said, "And Mr. Rose, you don't give me next month rent, okay?"

He was not expecting this from her. When it came to money, she was a hard woman to deal with.

"Thank you," he finally said. "I hope everything works out for your son."

Rhodes meant every word of it.

## THIRTY-EIGHT

Chris knocked on the door and held his breath. He was wearing a black tuxedo with recently polished dress shoes. He was also wearing a silver watch his dad had given him on his graduation.

He adjusted his tie and stretched his shirt collar. He was sweating so much that his shirt was stuck to his back. He hoped the sweat did not show on his face.

In his hand were twelve white roses. He was not sure red was appropriate. *It's not like it's Valentine's Day*, he thought. *And what if she thought red roses were my gesture of love? She'd kill me.*

He did not want to come across as too desperate or anxious. He wanted to be suave and sophisticated. He had to play it smooth as if he did not really care how the night turned out.

In reality, he cared too much, and it was messing him up. His mind was telling him, *Run. Put the roses on the door and leave. Don't even bother waiting for the elevators. Take the stairs and don't look back.*

*But if I do that, I will have to explain to Irina what happened.*

Chris gulped.

*And to the rest of the team, too.*

He knew Irina would be furious. According to Tarik, she would take Chris standing her up personally. He did not want to deal with the wrath of a woman, especially one who could bench-press a hundred pounds. She would eat him for breakfast, lunch, and dinner, and she would spit whatever was left of him in front of the FBI building.

A voice jolted him out of his thoughts. "You okay?"

Irina was holding the door. She was staring at him.

"You looked spaced out for a good minute or two," she said. She was wearing jeans, a white blouse, and a leather jacket. Pretty much the same attire she wore to work.

Chris blinked and tried to smile, but it came across as creepy.

Irina looked him over. "Why are you dressed like a waiter?"

"Um." He patted his gelled hair. "It's an important night, so I thought something more appropriate was in order."

He held the roses for her.

"What's this?" she asked.

"They're for you."

"Why?"

Chris swallowed. "I thought you might like them."

She stared at him and then grabbed the flowers. "Thanks. I'll put them inside."

When they reached his car, Chris quickly ran over and opened the passenger door for Irina.

She gave him a weird look but got in.

Chris drove a beat-up Honda Civic. It had over two hundred thousand miles on it, but it was still going. The air conditioner had stopped working long ago, but luckily, it was cool outside that night.

Chris leaned over and rolled down the window for her. He then realized he should not have because he had intruded into her space.

"Sorry," he said, quickly starting the engine.

During the drive, they did not say a word.

Chris found himself even more nervous than before. Irina looked stunning and he wanted to stare at her, but he was too afraid. He was not sure what was different about her that night. It was not like she had on a dress or even any makeup for that matter. Maybe it was the fact that she was sitting so close to him. He could literally lean over and kiss her. *Not that I would dare*, he thought. *She would snap my neck in two*.

He gripped the steering wheel tight. His palms were wet. He wanted to dry his hands on his pants but did not. He did not want to give away how nervous he was.

"You okay?" Irina asked again.

He gave her a weak smile. "Yeah, why wouldn't I be?"

"You look even paler than you normally do."

"I'm just excited."

She looked out the window.

At the restaurant, Irina looked around and said, "You got us reservations here?"

It was one of the priciest restaurants in Bridgeton, but it was also one of the hardest to get a table on short notice. Chris had to bribe the maître d' with cash in order to get a reservation, eating up a chunk of what was in his bank account.

"I know people, so I made a few calls," he claimed.

Once they were seated, a waiter came over and handed them menus. "To start, would you like to order some wine?" he asked.

"We'll have your special," Chris replied.

The waiter gave him a once-over and said, "Right away, sir."

Irina leaned over. "It's over three hundred dollars. Are you sure?"

"Of course," Chris said. "I want only the best for tonight."

At Chris's insistence, for starters, they ordered a seafood platter, which consisted of fresh fish, Gulf shrimp, and sea scallops marinated in lemon and white wine.

For entrées, Irina ordered a dish of sautéed veal with wild mushrooms, roasted red peppers, and spring onions. Chris ordered boneless chicken breast filled with fresh spinach and mushrooms, crowned with Mornay Sauce.

For dessert, Irina ordered a piece of red velvet cake filled with cream cheese and garnished with dark chocolate sprinkles. Chris ordered a decadent chocolate cake topped with chocolate frosting and whipped cream. They did not talk much. Chris was too nervous.

Chris finally signaled the waiter and said, "I am ready for the bill."

When the waiter handed Chris the slip, he glanced at it and his eyes widened.

He looked up and found Irina staring at him. He gave her a weak smile and then shoved his hand in his jacket pocket. He slowly began counting his money until he realized he did not have enough cash.

He pulled out his credit card.

"Stop," Irina said.

Chris looked up at her. "What?"

"Tarik put you up to it, didn't he?" she asked.

"I don't know what you mean."

"Don't lie to me. He told you to wine and dine me, didn't he?"

"Um… I kind of asked for his opinion. I wanted to make this night special."

She looked at him and then smiled. "Chris, I appreciate you doing all this for me, and I can honestly tell you you're the first guy who went out of his way to impress me. Most guys would've taken me to a bar or a fast food joint, thinking I'm not girly enough to want to go to a fancy restaurant. But let me tell you a secret: All girls—deep down—want to be treated like a princess. So thank you."

Chris was dumbfounded.

"Let me pay my half of the bill," she offered.

"But, I wanted to take you out," he said.

"You did take me out, and I really enjoyed the meal, but this place is way too high for both our salaries. If you let me pay my share, I'll let you buy me coffee afterward."

A smile came over Chris's face. "Really?"

"Sure," Irina replied. "It's not every day a guy shows up at my door wearing a tuxedo with flowers in his hand. Plus, this restaurant was a good choice. Did Tarik tell you about it?"

"No, I spent three hours searching online."

Her smile widened. "Stuff like that will make a girl feel special, you know."

Chris was beaming. For the first time that night, he was no longer nervous.

## THIRTY-NINE

Jo pulled a cardboard box out of a pile of boxes stored in her basement. All the boxes contained her parents' belongings.

She opened the box. The VHS tape was stuck in between other videotapes and audio recordings. She knew the tape was there because she had put it away after her mother had moved out of the house.

She turned on the old TV/VHS combo stored in the corner of the basement, pulled up a chair, and inserted the tape.

The first recording was of a family trip to the beach. Jo was only four years old, and she was scared to go into the water. Her father was holding the camera, and he was encouraging her to take a step further, saying, "It's all right, honey."

"Come on, Jo!" Sam yelled from the surf. He was already in chest-deep.

Her mother was lounging on a chair with the sun shining on her face, and she was smiling.

Her father placed the camera on the sand, ran up, and held her hand. Together they went into the water. Never once did he leave her side.

Jo fast-forwarded the tape.

The next recording was taken at home when they were celebrating Jo's birthday. The entire living room was adorned with balloons and other decorations. The view moved to the kitchen. Jo was seated at the dining table. Her father was manning the camera once again, and he focused on her face. Jo was pouting. Her father asked, "Why are you pouting, sweetie?" But Jo did not reply. Just then, Sam's voice could be heard in the background. Jo wanted the latest toy on the market, but she was told they could not find it. Jo was upset by this. Then, as if out of thin air, her father produced the toy and asked, "I wonder whose birthday it is?" Jo's eyes lit up. "It's *my* birthday, daddy," she replied over and over.

Her mother appeared holding a cake. The candles were already lit. They sang "Happy Birthday" and Jo blew out the candles.

Jo fast-forwarded to another home movie. This one was unsteady, and she immediately knew it was Sam holding the camera. He was showing off his action figurines. He then moved around his bedroom, pointing to all the comic book posters on the walls. He took the camera and walked around the house. He moved past Jo's room, where she was busy playing with her dolls. He then went downstairs. He moved around the living room until he reached the kitchen. Their mom was standing in the corner, crying. The moment she saw Sam, she said in a trembling voice, "Put that away, Sam."

The recording cut off.

Jo realized it was around this time that her mother had started to withdraw. She hardly ever smiled, and she had begun to spend more of her time in her garden. She had probably found out about her father's affair.

Jo could not believe she never picked up on it. She always assumed her mother fell into depression after her father's death, not during his lifetime. Even if Jo knew what was going on at that time, would she have believed her father was capable of hurting her mother?

Her mother had always been fragile, prone to emotional breakdowns. Her father, on the other hand, was like a rock. In many ways, her parents were different people, but they loved each other. Jo could see this whenever they were together. Her father would always say, "I can't believe a girl like her married a guy like me."

*Then why did he cheat on her?* Jo thought.

There was only one person who could answer that question.

# FORTY

Walters was silent when Jo confronted her.

They were in Walters's office. Jo was seated across from her. Jo had arrived early. She knew what time Walters came in. Jo did not want the team to see that she had returned from her leave. They would have a lot of questions for her, and she was in no mood to answer any of them.

"Who told you?" Walters slowly asked.

"Sam."

Walters looked down at her desk and nodded.

"Why didn't you tell me?" Jo asked.

"The same reason Sam never told you," she replied.

"I should've known."

"What good would it have done?" Walters said.

"At least I wouldn't have carried a lie with me all these years."

Walters sighed. "I wanted to tell you when you were old enough, but I wasn't sure how to do it. You adored your father. I didn't want to break your heart. Plus, I knew your condition, and I knew the kind of impact it would have on you if you found out. As time went by, I thought it was behind me. I was surprised when you showed up at my door, wanting to become a federal agent just like your father. I tried to discourage you, but you were determined to follow in his footsteps." Walters paused to gather her thoughts. "What happened between your father and me was wrong. It not only hurt your mother, it also destroyed my marriage. What you have to understand is that your father and I were under a lot of stress. The Bridgeton Ripper was the biggest thing that had gripped the city at that time. The case was all over the headlines. You may not know this, but I was also involved in the case. I was kept in the background, though. Twenty years ago, female agents were not given the spotlight. There weren't that many, to begin with. Your father disagreed with the way I was treated in the Bureau, but in order to please the upper brass, he kept quiet. It was another reason why he so badly wanted to catch the Ripper. He wanted to show his superiors that a woman could be just as instrumental as a male agent in helping catch a killer. Unfortunately, I was not aware of his whereabouts on the night of his death. Had I known he was in pursuit of the Ripper, I would have joined him. I regret not being there for him as his partner."

"And his lover," Jo shot back.

Walters was not offended. "The pressure of the Ripper case was too much for both of us. In a moment of weakness, we made a mistake. But I promise you, it never happened again. Your father was a good man. He loved you and he loved your brother very much. Believe it or not, he also loved your mother very much. And he always regretted how his infidelity destroyed her. I tried to make it up to your mother. Every week, I—"

She paused.

Jo understood. "You were the one who sent her flowers." Someone had been anonymously mailing tulips to her mother for years.

"I knew how much she loved red tulips. Your father mentioned it on many occasions, so I made sure she always had them to remind her of the good times in her life."

"Nothing reminds her of anything," Jo said. Her voice was bitter.

"I tried to meet her, to contact her, but she wanted nothing to do with me, and when her illness showed up, there was nothing more I could do that would make up for what happened. I'm sorry, Jo. I'm sorry that I didn't tell you. I should have, and I didn't. You can hate me all you want, but it takes two people to have an affair, and believe me, neither of us was very proud of it."

*She's right*, Jo thought. *If I am going to be mad at her, I have to be mad at dad too.*

Someone knocked on the door.

"Not now!" Walters said.

There was another knock.

"What is it?!" she yelled.

The door swung open and Tarik stuck his head in. "There is something on the news. You have to see it."

Walters and Jo left the room and found everyone staring at the large, flat-screen TV monitor on the wall. The female reporter on the screen was saying, "Someone claiming to be responsible for the deaths of George Moll and Kyle Summers has contacted BN-24. This person has indicated that he is providing justice to all those who have been wronged. For those not familiar, George Moll served a minimum sentence for the death of Joe Russo. Mr. Moll's body was found inside a hardware store that was once owned by Joe Russo. Kyle Summers was accused but never charged for the rape of Amy Lange. Mr. Summers's body was found in the backyard of Ms. Lange's home."

Jo's eyes narrowed.

"The person further mentioned another name: Mathias Lotta. Mr. Lotta is in the custody of the FBI. He is believed to be responsible for numerous deaths, including those dubbed the 'Motel Murders.' Mr. Lotta is currently in a coma at the Bridgeton General Hospital. The person has stated that if the FBI doesn't pull Lotta off life support, he will kill again, but this time it will be the FBI who'll be responsible for another death."

"I'm going to the hospital," Walters said, heading for the elevators.

"I'm coming too," Jo said.

"No chance," Walters said. "You're supposed to be on leave."

"And you were supposed to tell me what happened between you and my father."

Walters paused and stared at her.

"Fine," Walters said. "God knows we can use all the help we can get right now."

## FORTY-ONE

When they reached the hospital, they spotted a small group of protestors outside the main entrance. They were holding signs and chanting, "Let him die! Let him die!"

"It's already begun," Walters said.

"We'll go around to the back," Jo said. As they drove past the group, Jo read the signs they were waving.

*Murderer!*
*Serial Killer!*
*Monster!*

Jo could not disagree with them. Mathias had killed many people without remorse. He had an agenda, and in order to achieve it, he killed indiscriminately. In fact, he had made sure to dispose of anyone who got in his way—except her. He had spared her life when he could have put a bullet through her head. Why did he not do it? Did he have feelings for her? Did he actually care for her? Or did he feel some form of connection with her because they both had lost parents to the Bridgeton Ripper?

Jo was not sure, and she desperately needed answers. The only way for that to occur was if Mathias woke up. But now someone had made it his mission to prevent that from happening.

They parked, identified themselves to the policemen stationed outside the lobby, and headed inside.

They took the staff elevators up to the critical care unit, rushed down the hall, and were greeted by the officer stationed outside the room.

"Did anyone go in?" Walters asked.

The officer shook his head. "No one's gone in or out, ma'am."

"Good."

Jo went in. Mathias was in the same position as when she last visited. She scanned one monitor. He was alive and still breathing.

But he would not live for long if the crowd outside got their way.

She could hear their chants wafting up from the street below. She moved to the window and could see that more people had gathered in front of the hospital. Jo feared that soon the entire city would be pounding at the hospital's doors.

Walters came in, followed by a man in a white lab coat.

"I would advise against moving him," the doctor said. "His condition is already unstable. Anything we do could adversely affect him."

"We have no choice," Walters said. "We've already had someone try to kill him before. If we don't move him to a secure location, one or two officers stationed by his door would be no use if a mob decided to storm this unit."

The doctor looked at his patient and then heard the cries of protest from outside. "I'll put in a request for his move."

## FORTY-TWO

Tarik and Irina arrived at BN-24. They were greeted by Miles Stevenson, the 24-hour news channel's producer. Miles was tanned, with dark hair and a chiseled jaw. He looked a little weary when he spoke. "Thanks for coming. Right after we aired the segment, I called you guys."

"You should've called us right when you'd received the email," Tarik said.

"We didn't have time," Miles said. "This person sent the same email to other news outlets, and if we didn't jump on it first, they would've."

"Why *did* you call us?" Irina asked, curious.

He looked at her. "You don't remember what happened to Ellen?" he replied.

Ellen Sheehan was a star reporter for BN-24, and she had worked under Miles. Ellen had started receiving calls from a person claiming to be responsible for the Train Killings. Someone was leaving dismembered bodies on subway trains for passengers to find. Ellen made the mistake of pursuing the killer in the hope of gaining exclusive access to him. This turned out to be fatal, for she was shot in the back of her head while leaving work late one night. There was no link between the real Train Killer—Craig Orton—and Ellen's death, as Orton was captured and killed prior to her demise. But Miles strongly believed Ellen knew too much and that someone wanted her gone.

Miles said, "My main concern is the well-being of my reporters."

He escorted the two agents to his office, where a woman was waiting for them. She was dressed in a white blouse, a green jacket and skirt, and heels.

"Sarita Kapoor," Miles said, introducing her. Tarik and Irina recognized her as the reporter they saw on TV. She had a brown complexion, short, cropped hair, and dark eyes. "Sarita was the one who received the email."

"Can we see it?" Tarik asked.

She opened her laptop and let them view it.

"How do you know if it's the real killer?" Irina asked.

"Look how long the email is," Sarita replied. "This person goes into great detail about how he murdered George Moll and Kyle Summers. Naturally, we tried to verify this with the Bureau, but no one would speak to us."

The FBI preferred to keep information about ongoing cases out of the press. There were instances where it was necessary to use the press to further an investigation, but that was only done when they felt there were no other options.

Sarita said, "So we phoned one of our contacts in the Bridgeton PD, and he was able to confirm most of what the killer had claimed in the email."

"We'll have to analyze the email to see if there is anything that might help us track who sent it," Tarik said. "Do you mind if I forward it to one of our IT specialists at the bureau?"

"No, go ahead."

While Tarik worked on her laptop, Miles said, "Should I be concerned for my reporters?"

Irina said, "Unless the killer has made a direct threat against anyone, I wouldn't worry too much."

Miles did not look convinced.

# FORTY-THREE

The press had gathered outside the hospital, and it looked like every news channel, newspaper, and blogger was there. This case had suddenly become *the* most talked-about story in the city. Someone claiming to be the killer had given the police and the FBI an ultimatum: end the life of a serial killer, or else another person would meet the same fate as George Moll and Kyle Summers.

In order to avoid mass hysteria, Walters had decided to go meet the press. She wanted to reassure the public that the FBI was taking this threat very seriously.

Jo had tried to talk Walters out of it. She felt this was exactly what the killer had wanted: an audience. The way he displayed his victims' bodies indicated he was seeking attention. With Walters talking about him, he would get even more exposure. The more people talked about him, the more empowered he would become.

But Walters would not be dissuaded. She did not want the killer to think the FBI was somehow hiding. No one was above the law, and no *one* person would dictate what a federal law agency would or would not do.

Jo watched from a distance as Walters walked out the front of the hospital and approached a circle of reporters.

The moment she opened her mouth, hands shot up in the air.

She pointed to one reporter.

"What are you doing to stop this killer?" the reporter asked.

"All our resources have been dedicated to finding the person behind these recent murders," Walters answered.

"Why not just pull the plug and avoid another death?" a second reporter asked.

"We don't kill people because someone tells us to. Plus, Mathias Lotta is responsible for multiple deaths, and it is our duty to bring him before a jury so that they may choose his fate."

Another reporter said, "Isn't it true that the Bridgeton PD blames the FBI for Detective Crowder's death?"

"I can't confirm something that I'm not aware of."

The same reporter said, "Chief Baker has gone on record and said if the Bridgeton PD was on the Motel Murders case, Detective Crowder would still be alive."

"What happened to Detective Crowder was nothing short of a tragedy. Not a day goes by that my team and I don't regret not catching Mathias Lotta sooner. We all wish Detective Crowder was with us right now."

Another hand shot up. "Ten minutes ago, Chief Baker made a comment to the press that if he was in charge, he would be willing to negotiate with the killer in order to prevent harm to an innocent person."

Jo would not be surprised if Baker had actually said that. From the moment Mathias was brought into the hospital, Baker was adamant that he be left to die. Baker had nothing but contempt for Mathias. If shooting a murderer was legal, he would do so in a heartbeat.

Walters said, "It is true that the FBI and the Bridgeton PD's relationship is currently strained, but I don't think the Bridgeton PD would concede to the demands of a killer. I would hope the chief would want us to find the person who is making this threat and put him behind bars."

Jo could tell the questioning had taken on an ugly tone. The media was pitting two law enforcement agencies against each other. Baker had thrown the first volley with his comments, and they were hoping Walters would serve back. So far, she was not taking the bait.

Martin Rhodes emerged from the crowd and approached Jo. "I saw it on the news and I rushed over," he said. "How is Mathias doing?"

Rhodes was at the water facility the night Mathias was shot. Rhodes agreed with Jo that there was more to this story than what they saw that night. Mathias wanted to confess, and they felt he was prevented from doing so.

"His condition is critical *and* unstable," she said.

"What if he doesn't make it?" he asked.

Jo frowned. It was a question she had asked her a million times. "Then there is nothing more we can do about it. He'll take all his secrets with him to the grave."

# FORTY-FOUR

Chris was able to track the IP address the killer had used. It came from a local library. They were not sure if the killer had actually used a library computer. The email may have been routed from somewhere else. Tarik thought it would be best if Irina and Chris checked it out for themselves.

Irina drove while Chris sat in the passenger seat with his laptop.

"I had a great time last night," Irina said.

Chris smiled. "Me too."

"I'm not saying we should be a couple or anything, but if you want to hang out again, I'm cool with it."

"That sounds good," Chris said, breathing a sigh of relief. He realized the night before that even though he was attracted to her, she was not the one for him. She obviously knew it way before him. He had been too enamored with her to think otherwise.

She was a fantasy and nothing more. He dreamed of wanting to be with her, but when he had the chance, he understood that they were completely different people. They did not share the same interests or hobbies. Plus, what she wanted in life was the complete opposite of what he wanted.

Irina was not interested in marriage or children. She wanted a partner, but nothing that was long-term. Instead, she wanted a pet that would not demand too much of her life. She wanted to be free to travel and explore the world.

Chris, on the other hand, dreamed of having a wife and a couple of children. He grew up in a loving household and he wanted to establish one of his own. He wanted to play video games with his children and go out on movie dates with his wife. Stability and security was something he craved.

They pulled up in front of a Victorian-style building.

The moment they entered the library, they were hit with pure silence. Every once in a while, a page would flip or someone would cough, but apart from that, the place was eerily quiet.

Irina sighed. "I hate libraries. They put me to sleep."

"I actually like them," Chris said. "They are filled with so much knowledge."

"Boring," Irina said.

*That's another reason why we're incompatible*, Chris thought.

They approached the main desk, and Irina flashed her credentials to the woman seated there. "Someone sent an email from one of your computers. We're trying to find out who it was."

The librarian seemed stumped. "Um... okay, sure. What is it you want to know?"

"Do you have security cameras?" Irina asked.

The librarian shook her head. "With all the budget cuts, we can barely afford to update our computers."

"Where are your computers?" Chris asked.

The librarian pointed to the other side of the room. There were three desktops with people already seated before them.

"How would someone come and use them?" Irina asked.

"What do you mean?" the librarian asked.

"Do they need a library card, for instance?"

She nodded. "Yes. And they have to reserve a time for the computer."

"How would they do that?" Irina asked.

"We have a sign-in book."

The librarian slid a binder in front of them.

Irina turned to Chris. "What time was the email sent?"

Chris opened his computer and pulled up the email Tarik had forwarded from BN-24. "It was in the morning, around nine thirty-seven."

Irina moved her finger down the list and then stopped. The handwriting was illegible, but there was a library card number next to the signature.

"Can you find out who the card belongs to?" Irina asked.

The librarian looked up the number. "Frederick Joseph."

"Do you have an address?"

The librarian checked and then frowned.

"What's wrong?" Irina asked.

"It's a PO box," she replied. "We don't accept those."

"Thanks anyway."

Back in the car, Chris typed furiously on his computer. "I'll check all the databases. If there is a Frederick Joseph, we'll find him."

A minute later, he said, "Damn."

"What?" Irina asked.

"Frederick Joseph is dead."

"I knew it was too good to be true."

"But…"

Chris's voice trailed off.

"But what?" Irina asked anxiously.

"You wouldn't believe when he died, and how."

"Okay, tell me."

"Frederick Joseph died almost twenty years ago. He was the first victim of the Bridgeton Ripper."

Irina put the car in gear. "We need to tell Walters," she said.

## FORTY-FIVE

Jo and Walters were in the hallway of the hospital when Irina and Chris told them what they had found.

Walters said, "Frederick Joseph? It doesn't make any sense."

"Actually, it does," Jo said.

"How?"

"Mathias was interested in the Bridgeton Ripper case. His mother was the Ripper's last victim. Whoever is behind these latest killings must have read the articles on Mathias after we had caught him. He's probably using information from the case to lead us on a wild goose chase."

Walters frowned. "It doesn't help us find who's doing this."

"I think I might know," a voice said.

They did not realize Rhodes was also in the hallway.

Walters frowned. "This is an FBI-only meeting," she said.

"Just listen to me," Rhodes said. "Someone wants Mathias dead. Did you ask yourself why?"

"It's quite obvious," Walters replied. "This person, in his twisted mind, is killing people he believes were not punished appropriately for their crimes. George Moll, Kyle Summers, and even Mathias Lotta had either not served enough time in prison or had not served any time at all."

"Okay, fine, but why now?" Rhodes asked.

Walters shrugged. "Why does anyone kill? They're either lusting for blood, or they have an agenda."

"Exactly," Rhodes said. "Whoever is behind this has an agenda, and they've planned this out very methodically. I believe the deaths of Moll and Summers were only a setup."

"For what?"

"To force us to give up Mathias Lotta."

Walters shook her head. "I don't buy it."

"Think about it. Someone had previously attempted to kill Mathias. What you need to ask yourself is who would want him dead?"

Walters exhaled. "Maybe it was someone from his victims' families. Maybe it was someone who he had crossed paths with. Maybe—"

"Maybe it was his father," Rhodes suggested.

"What?" Walters and Jo asked in unison.

"Yes. Dr. Lotta hired me to find his son when all evidence indicated he was dead. For a long time, I couldn't understand why until I realized it had something to do with the Train Killings. Silvio Tarconi, Natasha Wedham, and Doug Curran were responsible for tormenting Mathias at the Bridgeton Mental Care Institute. They did so on the instructions of Dr. Lotta. During my investigation on Mathias, I uncovered payments from Dr. Lotta to all three individuals. I confronted Dr. Lotta about that, but he indicated the payments were for them to take care of his son, not torment him. Also, prior to Mathias being admitted to the institute, he had gone to the police and told them his father was trying to kill him. Dr. Lotta was questioned, and he stated that his son had had a psychotic episode and had not taken his medication. Up until then, Mathias had never shown any signs of erratic or even dangerous behavior."

"Get to the point, Mr. Rhodes," Walters said impatiently.

"The victims of the Motel Murders were all men who were bad husbands, bad fathers, or both. This was a message from Mathias to his father, whom he considered a bad father for sending him to the institute and a bad husband for not protecting his mother from the Bridgeton Ripper."

Walters shook her head again. "It's too farfetched."

"Also, it was Dr. Lotta who shot his son right before he was able to tell us why he was doing all this in the first place."

"These are serious allegations," Walters said. "Dr. Lotta is a respected physician in Bridgeton. On top of that, he is a great supporter of the Bridgeton PD. I have met him at several charitable events, which, by the way, he was hosting."

"Bring Dr. Lotta in for questioning," Rhodes insisted. "I don't think all of this is just a coincidence."

Walters stared at him. She was debating whether to believe him or throw him out for spreading conspiracies.

Irina said, "Can I add something?"

"What?" Walters turned to her.

"When Tarik and I were at Kyle Summers's apartment complex, we spoke to one of his neighbors, and he said on the night Summers disappeared, he overheard him crying in his apartment. He also heard him mention a doctor."

"Are you sure?" Walters asked.

Irina nodded. "The neighbor clearly stated this. You can confirm it with Tarik if you like."

Walters stared at Jo, Irina, Chris, and then Rhodes.

She finally said, "Fine. We'll bring Dr. Lotta in, but *I'll* question him."

Tarik jogged up to them. "We've got a bigger problem now."

They all rushed to a waiting room. Staff had already gathered around a wall-mounted TV.

On the screen, a woman was in front of a camera. The wall behind her was dark, but her face was clearly visible, as if someone was shining a strong light on her. She was in tears. Her mascara streaked down her cheeks.

"My name is Emily Bennett… I am married to Steven Bennett and I have two children. Kaley is seven and Konner is five… I love my children and I love my husband..." She controlled her emotions and continued. "I am being held against my will. I don't know by whom, but if Mathias Lotta is not dead by sunrise… I… I will be the next victim… please help me…"

She broke down. "Please save me… I'm begging you…"

The screen went blank.

"Oh, dear God," Walters said.

They were all thinking the same thing.

# FORTY-SIX

It was chaos outside the hospital. What was once a couple of dozen people was now over a hundred. There were fears that soon it would be a thousand, and then all hell would break loose. Police had already blocked off all entrances and exits to the hospital. No visitors were allowed, and only staff and people with emergencies were permitted inside.

The protestors were chanting, "Let him die! Save Emily! Let him die! Save Emily!"

Claire Gilkin stared out the window in apprehension. Her hair that was once auburn was now gray, her skin that was once smooth and tight was now sagging and covered with blotches, and her figure that was once slim was now heavy. This was the price she had to pay to become the hospital administrator. She had started working at the hospital thirty years earlier as a secretary for one of the doctors. She worked her way up to becoming the first female to hold an executive position.

The year before, she ran her first fundraising campaign, and she was able to raise over fifty million in donations for the hospital. She had three more years to go before she retired, and she hoped she would have a lasting influence at the hospital. In fact, she wished that the board would one day name a wing in her name. Something like, "The Claire Gilkin Cardiac Care Unit."

Suddenly, after eighteen months on the job, she had a sinking feeling that all her hard work would be wasted. There would be nothing named after her if she did something that could tarnish the hospital's reputation and jeopardize the well-being of its staff.

"This is getting out of hand," she said.

"I agree," a voice said. Chief Vincent Baker was tall and imposing, but his large gut was barely held in by his uniform. The moment the situation worsened, he had rushed over to the hospital and made himself available to the administrator. "But unfortunately, my hands are tied."

She turned to him. "Can't you remove Mr. Lotta and take him to another location?"

"I wish I could, but he is under FBI jurisdiction."

"Wasn't one of their agents romantically involved with Mr. Lotta?"

"Yes."

"And wasn't one of your detectives killed by Mr. Lotta?"

Baker's brow furrowed. "Yes. What's your point?"

"Can't you talk to someone higher up about this? Maybe call the mayor or even the governor if you have to."

Baker was silent. He hated having to give up control to any agency, especially the FBI. Their relationship had gone from strained to nonexistent. Baker knew he should not have made his incendiary comments regarding Lotta to the press. He got enough flak for them from his superiors. But he had made his remarks right after Crowder's death. He was in shock, and his emotions had gotten the better of him. But whatever he said to the media, he still stood by his words.

The FBI should have handed Lotta over to the Bridgeton PD a long time ago. An agent of theirs was in a relationship with the killer, and this killer had taken the life of one of his officers. But the FBI was a federal agency, and they had authority over Lotta.

What Gilkin had suggested to him was tantamount to career suicide. If he jumped ranks and contacted officials higher up without the board's knowledge, his superiors would have his head.

Gilkin said, "I know I'm putting you in a difficult position, but I have a building filled with patients and health-care providers. We need to be able to get ambulances safely in and out of the hospital. If we can't function properly, we are putting people's lives in danger." She turned back to the window. "Just listen to the crowd. They want justice. And if we don't give it to them, I fear they will take matters into their own hands."

There was a long silence between them.

"Let me see what I can do," Baker finally said.

## FORTY-SEVEN

When Tarik showed up at Ansel Lotta's house, the doctor put up no resistance. In fact, he was more than accommodating to Tarik's request.

Lotta entered the interview room dressed in a three-piece suit. He was also carrying his briefcase, which he placed next to the table.

"Thank you for coming, Dr. Lotta," Walters said.

"I can't say it's my pleasure, but I'm here."

Jo and Rhodes were in another room. They could hear and see everything behind the two-way mirror. Rhodes had been given permission to listen in. He had a feeling the only reason Walters allowed it was to prove to him that he was wrong about Lotta.

Walters took a seat across from Lotta and said, "I do apologize for this sudden meeting, but I would like to ask you a few questions."

"Do I need a lawyer?" Lotta asked.

"You can have one… it is your right, but you have not been charged with anything."

"Then, why am I here?"

"We would like to clarify certain things."

Lotta stared at her. "All right, fine."

"Where were you yesterday?" Walters asked.

"That's simple. I was at my clinic."

"All day?"

"Yes. You can ask my secretary."

"What about your patients?"

"What about them?"

"Did you see any?"

"Of course, I did. I can give you a list of the patients' names, but I'm afraid I can't discuss anything personal. Doctor-patient privileges, I hope you understand."

"We're not interested in your patients. We just want to verify your whereabouts for the entire day."

Lotta sighed. "I'm a respected surgeon…"

"I'm fully aware of that, and again I apologize for this, but it is necessary."

"Does this have anything to do with my son?" Lotta asked.

Walters did not say anything.

"Is this about all that stuff on TV?"

"Yes, someone wants your son dead, and we want to know why."

"And you think it's me?"

"Someone believes so, yes."

Rhodes knew she was referring to him.

Lotta smiled. "I know how this looks. I searched for my son, and I ended up shooting him. But if I remember correctly, my son had murdered at least three people. I would have preferred my son was not in a coma but in a treatment facility getting better. However, that's not how things worked out, unfortunately."

"What's your connection to the Bridgeton Ripper?" Walters asked.

Lotta paused. "I haven't had someone ask me that in a long time. It's actually very simple. My wife—Mathias's mother—was his last victim."

"I know you've answered this before, but where were you on the night your wife disappeared? I mean, the night she was taken by the Bridgeton Ripper?"

Lotta sighed. "Like I told the police years ago, I was at home with my son."

"Do you have any motive to harm your son?"

"I might."

Walters looked surprised. "And why is that?"

"He did, after all, try to kill me and hurt my family."

"But it is *he* who is in a coma and not *you*, isn't that right?"

Lotta nodded. "Yes." He leaned forward. "I understand the FBI is under a lot of stress. It can't be easy having a madman out there threatening to kill a woman with a husband and two young children. I saw the footage on TV."

Walters paused and stared at him. She said, "What would you do in our position? Would you concede to this madman's demands?"

Lotta's eyes narrowed. "I know what you're trying to do. You want me to say that I would pull the plug and let Mathias die, isn't that correct?"

"I'm only asking for your opinion."

Lotta crossed his arms. "Frankly, I wouldn't give in to a killer's demands. Who's to say he wouldn't kill the woman after you let Mathias die?"

"This is something we have considered."

"But then, if you don't do anything and the woman dies, what will you tell her family? How would you face them? They'll surely blame you for not doing enough to save their loved one."

Walters was silent.

Lotta looked at his watch. "I'm sorry, but I have patients waiting for me at my clinic. If you have some evidence against me, then please bring it forward, but if you are fishing for something, you are wasting your time."

Walters stared at him for a few seconds. "Thank you for coming, Dr. Lotta. I apologize for the inconvenience," she said, rising to her feet to shake hands with him.

When Lotta was gone, Walters turned and looked directly at the mirror. Rhodes could feel her looking at him. Rhodes had a feeling Walters would not give him another chance to prove his theory, but he did not buy Lotta's claims.

## FORTY-EIGHT

Rhodes drove straight home. He knew even if Lotta was not lying, he was hiding something.

Rhodes knew full well he did not have any concrete evidence to link Lotta to what was going on, but the doctor had the means and opportunity. He had paid three people at the mental institute to torment his son. He could have easily hired someone to kill George Moll and Kyle Summers and was now holding Emily Bennett hostage.

But that was all conjecture and nothing more. Rhodes simply had acted on strong gut instinct. He knew when to trust his intuition.

Walters had given him a piece of her mind. "Mr. Rhodes, we are trying to find a killer. We can't waste time suspecting innocent people," she had said, giving him a hard look.

"Dr. Lotta is not innocent," Rhodes had wanted to say. "He has blood on his hands. He was the one who shot his son, whom he always wanted dead. I believe he is willing to do anything to finish the job." But he had kept quiet.

Rhodes grunted.

He was becoming obsessed with a case again, which had been his undoing before. All he saw was red. He could not explain this to anyone because they would not understand. He could not shake a strong feeling that told him something was not right.

Maybe he needed a break after going on all cylinders for days. There had been the matter with Yevgeny, and then Paco had shown up. This was on top of Mac's case, which he was still looking into. And then there was Sully's upcoming wedding. He still had not checked out the suit the old man had left for him. But he could not complain. He had spent ten years mostly sitting idle in a cramped prison cell, an ordeal that nearly made him lose his mind. He was attracted to chaos and thrived in it, a trait he had acquired when he was young and living with a father who was always one step away from prison.

*I need a drink*, Rhodes thought.

He looked up and realized he was already at his apartment.

He parked the Malibu and got out.

When he reached the front door, he heard voices inside.

*Who the hell is here?* he thought.

He unlocked the door and entered.

He found Tess sitting on his sofa with a boy.

"What're you doing here?" Rhodes asked. "And who is he?"

The boy stood up and came over. He was wearing a corduroy jacket, black jeans, and blue high-tops. "I'm Simon," he said. "I'm Tess's co-worker."

"Co-worker?" Rhodes asked with surprise as he shook Simon's hand.

Tess gave Rhodes a weak smile. "You know how you asked me why I wasn't around as often? It's because I got a part-time job."

"Where?"

"The music shop down on Oak Street."

"Why didn't you tell me?"

"I didn't want anyone to find out, especially my mom, or else she'd make me help pay rent."

"Okay, but why is *he* in my apartment?" Rhodes asked, looking at Simon.

Tess said, "I told Simon about what you do and how you were behind Mathias Lotta's capture."

"I saw it on the news," Simon said with a smile.

"That still doesn't explain why he's in my apartment." Rhodes did not like people barging into his home. He had become prickly when it came to his privacy and space, luxuries he had not enjoyed for ten years. He had longed for a quiet space all his own, a place uninterrupted by the sounds of slamming cell doors and the voices of guards and inmates. "I want to help," Simon said.

"Help what?" Rhodes asked.

"Help find Emily Bennett."

Rhodes stared at him. "How will you do that?"

"Let me explain," Simon said. "Every night after I get off work, my buddies and I go down to the park to skateboard. Last night I heard a loud noise… like a gunshot."

"Did your friends hear it too?"

"Yeah, they did, but they thought it could be the sound of a tire going flat."

"But you thought differently?"

"Yeah, I know a gunshot when I hear one."

"How?"

"My dad owns a lot of guns, so I've been around them all my life."

"Okay, so how is this related to Emily Bennett?"

"On the news, they said Emily was driving an orange Fiat with a sunflower decal across the side door. It had something to do with her daughter liking sunflowers. Anyway, when I went to check on that gunshot last night, I saw a Fiat drive out of the street I heard the shot come from. It had a flowery design on the side."

Rhodes's eyes narrowed. "Did you tell this to the police or the FBI?"

"I called the police hotline and told them, but I couldn't tell if they took me seriously or not."

Rhodes figured the police were likely bombarded with hundreds of calls from people with information. Going through all those calls to find what was relevant and what was not would take time.

Simon said, "Anyway, I told Tess about it, and she brought me here."

"You think it's the same car?" Rhodes asked.

"I don't know." He glanced at Tess. Then he turned back to Rhodes. "You're the detective. You tell me."

Rhodes rubbed his chin.

"Can you take me there?" he asked.

## FORTY-NINE

Jo and Walters found Tarik waiting for them by the hospital's side entrance.

"Is he okay?" Walters asked immediately. The moment Tarik had called and told them to come back to the hospital, Walters kept thinking something had happened to Mathias.

"His condition hasn't changed," Tarik said, "but there's a new development. Come, I'll show you."

Tarik led them up the stairs, down a hall, and past several wards. Staff and patients eyed Walters with suspicion. They had seen her on TV and knew she was the person holding Emily Bennett's life in her hands. If she pulled the plug and let a killer meet the same fate as his victims, Emily could be back with her family. *It is not as simple as that*, Walters wanted to tell them. She could not let one person die just to save another. They did not hold power over who lived and who died. Their job was to ensure that everyone was protected from harm regardless of who they were and what they had done.

There was also the matter of letting a killer dictate what they should and should not do. If they conceded now, who was to say there would not be more copycat killers showing up in Bridgeton? And what if a gang or cartel held an innocent person hostage for the release of one of their comrades? It happened routinely in other countries, but not in the United States. The U.S. did not negotiate with terrorists. And Walters was not going to negotiate with killers. She was not going to open that door for others to take advantage of later on.

If people wanted to hate her for her stance, so be it.

From the third-floor window, Tarik pointed to the front of the hospital. Night had fallen, but the crowd outside had swelled. There were perhaps thousands of people reciting chants and holding signs.

A man was standing in front of the crowd with a bullhorn in his hand.

"Who is that?" Walters asked.

"The husband of the kidnapped woman," Tarik replied.

Walters sighed. "This will not be good."

The man raised the bullhorn to his mouth. "My name is Steven Bennett. I am married to Emily Bennett. Emily is a loving wife and a caring mother. I met Emily ten years ago at a friend's wedding. She was one of the bridesmaids, and I was one of the groomsmen. The moment I saw her, I knew I wanted to one day make her my bride. We've been married for nine years, and we have two wonderful children. Kaley is seven and Konner is five."

Walters knew what he was doing. By telling the crowd his story, he was bringing them on his side.

"Kaley and Konner miss their mother dearly. They are waiting for her at home. I miss my wife. I love her so much. I want my children to grow up with their mother at their side, and I want to grow old with my wife. I am begging the FBI to let that murderer die so that my wife can be with us again."

He lowered the bullhorn.

The crowd chanted, "Let him die! Save Emily!"

Walters sighed. "Bring him inside. We have to talk to him."

A few minutes later, an officer escorted Steven Bennett down the hall. He was dressed in a light sweater, jeans, and loafers. There was a day-old growth on his chin, and his eyes were red and puffy.

"Mr. Bennett," Walters said. "I'm Special Agent in Charge Charlotte Walters."

"I know who you are," he said. "I saw you on TV."

"Then you know why we can't give in to a killer's demands."

"I don't care for the reasons," he spat. "I just want my wife back."

"I understand this a difficult time for you."

"You have no idea what I'm going through," he said, raising his voice. "This is a nightmare I can't wake up from. The thought of my wife tied up in some dark hole is eating away at me. I feel helpless. I don't know where she is, and I can't help her."

"We are doing everything we can to find her."

Bennett's eyes flashed with rage. "You're not doing enough. In a few hours, she will be dead. I want my wife back!"

"You have to let us do our job," Walters said.

His face twisted into a scowl. "If you won't kill that bastard, let me do it."

"You'll go to jail for murder."

Bennett grunted. "That's better than waiting for my wife to die."

Walters was taken aback. *People will risk everything to save a loved one, including their freedom*, she thought.

"We'll find her," Walters said.

"Why is it that I don't trust you?" he said.

"You have no other choice, sir."

"Let him die!" he screamed as he lunged at her.

The officer grabbed him by the arms and dragged him away.

"Let him die!" Bennet kept screaming.

His voice echoed down the halls, adding an eerie accompaniment to the chants wafting up from the streets.

# FIFTY

Walters was shaken by her meeting with Mr. Bennett. She could see the pain in his eyes, and she felt sorry for him.

Walters turned to Jo and Tarik. "Anything on Mrs. Bennett?"

"I've contacted all the agencies in the city, and they're willing to allocate resources to help find her," Tarik said.

"She could be anywhere," Jo said. "Even with help, we have no idea where to look."

Chief Baker and Gilkin approached them.

"This has gotten out of hand," Gilkin said. "My staff can't enter or leave the hospital. They feel like hostages."

"They can leave the building at any time," Walters said. "Just as long as we can vet who enters and leaves."

"You have to get him out of here," Gilkin demanded. Her eyes were as hard as granite.

"You're going to risk the safety of a patient?" Walters asked.

"It's one patient's safety against the safety of hundreds of other patients and my staff."

"I can't allow you to discharge him."

"It's not your choice anymore," Gilkin said.

"What're you talking about?" Walters asked.

Baker spoke up. "I just got off the phone with the governor, and I've been given assurance that he will be having a word with your superiors."

As if on cue, Walters's phone rang.

"You might want to answer that," Baker said.

Walters did, and after a tense exchange, she hung up. "That was the director of the FBI," she said.

"And what did he have to say?" Baker asked.

"We are ordered to hand over the suspect to the Bridgeton PD."

Baker smiled.

"This isn't right, and you know that, Chief Baker," Jo said.

"The way Detective Crowder was murdered wasn't right either," Baker replied.

Jo glared at Baker. "If you move him, he'll die."

"Stop trying to protect your boyfriend," Baker shot back.

"This isn't about my relationship," Jo countered. "This is about giving in to the demands of a murderer."

"If you had let him die in the first place, we would not be in this situation," Baker said.

"How do you know for sure?" Jo replied. "If it wasn't Mathias Lotta, it could've been someone else. The last thing we need is to let a murderer destroy an ongoing investigation."

"What investigation?" Baker said. "Mathias Lotta was responsible for the Motel Murders. He was also responsible for murdering Crowder. He should get the death penalty for what he did."

"But his fate should not be decided by another murderer. His fate should be decided in court," Jo said. "I hope you haven't forgotten your responsibilities as an officer of the law."

Baker gave Jo a stern look. "He's now under our custody, and we'll decide what to do with him."

Jo was about to say something when Walters put her hand on her arm. "He's yours, Chief Baker," Walters said. "But if this goes south, believe me, I will use all of my powers to come down hard on you."

# FIFTY-ONE

Accompanied by Tess and Simon, Rhodes drove to where Simon had heard the gunshot.

Rhodes was not sure if their investigation would lead to anything, but it was worth a try. A woman's life was on the line. The last thing he wanted was to ignore something that could end up saving her.

"That's where my buddies and I go skateboarding," Simon said from the back seat. The concrete park was empty at this time of night. "And I saw the Fiat come out of there."

He pointed to a street up ahead.

They pulled into it. There were cars parked on one side of the street.

"Keep your eyes peeled for anything interesting," Rhodes said.

Tess sat next to him in the passenger seat. She rolled down her window and stuck her head out.

Rhodes slowed as they passed each parked vehicle. When they were at the end of the street, Rhodes said, "Simon, you heard the gunshot when you were skateboarding, is that right?"

"Yep," Simon replied.

Rhodes frowned. "We're too far away from the park. There's no way you could've heard anything from here."

He turned the Malibu around and drove back to the main road. "When the Fiat came out of this street, which direction did it go?" Rhodes asked.

"It turned left."

Locating one particular car among dozens of vehicles in the neighborhood would not be easy. *And whoever was driving the Fiat may have driven it to who-knows-where*, Rhodes thought.

He looked around for any security cameras. If he could find one, maybe in the morning, they would be able to access the footage and confirm whether the Fiat passed by or not.

*But Emily Bennett might not be alive by morning.*

"This is fun," Simon said. "Is this what you guys do when you are investigating?"

Tess smiled. "Yep, but it can get dangerous. I was held hostage by the Train Killer."

"No way. That was you?"

"Yep."

"Were you scared?"

She shrugged. "Kind of, but Martin saved me."

"Maybe I can join your team," Simon said.

"There is no team," Rhodes said.

Tess said, "Technically, Martin does all the work. I just help out. It's safer that way."

"Cool. I get it."

They had been driving for ten minutes when Rhodes decided it was time to head back. *Well, we gave it a shot*, he thought.

"Stop the car!" Simon yelled.

Rhodes hit the brakes. "What?"

"I think I saw something. You have to go back."

Rhodes looked around. The street was deserted.

"It's on the intersection you just passed,"
Simon said. Rhodes drove in reverse until Simon
pointed and said, "There!"

Next to the intersection was another street. On
that street was a lone, parked car.

Rhodes squinted. He could not make out the
model, but he could tell the vehicle was orange.

He turned the wheel and drove onto the street.
As they neared the car, he recognized it. The
sunflower decal was clearly visible.

Rhodes got out and approached the vehicle.
He peered inside and saw the car was empty.

A parking ticket was stuck to the windshield.

"What is it doing here?" Tess asked.

Rhodes did not know.

## FIFTY-TWO

Steven Bennett rubbed his chin and checked his watch. He was sitting in his car in the hospital's parking lot.

He needed a quiet place to calm his nerves. He took a sip of the vodka his brother had brought for him. His children were with his sister-in-law. They were anxious for their father to bring home their mother. And that was exactly what he was going to do.

*Damn SAC Walters*, he thought. *She does not care what happens to my wife. She only cares about what happens to that murderer.*

Steven had read about the murderer's relationship with another FBI agent. He felt Walters was protecting the murderer because of that agent.

He used to never believe in conspiracies, but now he was beginning to think differently. This was not about doing what was right, which would be to let a murderer die and save an innocent wife and mother. This was about the FBI saving face for what had happened with the Motel Murders. They desperately wanted the murderer to come out of his coma so he could be paraded in front of the cameras as he was put on trial. This way, they could show to the public that justice was served and a criminal was locked up because of their actions.

*Well, I'm not going to leave it in their hands*, he thought. *No. I'm going to do something about it.*

Fortunately, his brother owned a party supply store. He was familiar with fireworks, which he sold for the Fourth of July and other events.

Steven took another sip of vodka. After checking his watch again, he got out.

The crowd was still gathered by the front of the hospital. He was grateful for their support, but he needed more than chants and slogans to save his wife.

He walked around the side of the parking lot and headed straight for the emergency room entrance. Two police officers were standing by the doors, checking who came in and out. No visitors were permitted, only people with emergencies or critical care needs were allowed inside.

*All this trouble for a murderer*, he thought. *What a waste of resources.*

He checked his watch one more time. In less than a minute, his brother would drop a few of the fireworks inside a garbage container not far from where the large group had gathered. Once they went off, there would be chaos, giving him the opening he needed.

As if on cue, there was a loud bang, followed by several more. Then there was the sound of people screaming.

He watched as the two officers left their post to see what had happened.

Steven ran and was through the doors within seconds. He looked around and found two more officers on the other side of the emergency room. They were too preoccupied with a patient in handcuffs to notice him.

He quickly snuck past them and moved down the hall. He knew where he was going. He remembered where they had brought him when he came to meet Walters.

He took the elevator up, and when he got out, he could see the staff staring out the windows. They were probably wondering what was going on outside.

He found a linen closet and grabbed a white lab coat. He put it on and then raced to the critical care unit's registration desk. On the wall behind the desk was a whiteboard with patient names and room numbers written in black marker.

He found the number he was looking for and headed straight for the room.

He found no officer standing by the door. *They all must have gone to see what the commotion was about*, he thought. *Good, good.*

He entered the room and found a man lying on the bed. Wires were going from his body to the monitors next to him. Steven checked his vitals. The man was still alive.

Steven approached him. The man had graying hair and slight stubble. Steven was not sure if he was the murderer. The photo he had seen in the news was taken years ago when the murderer was in the mental care institute. *Maybe he aged over the years*, he thought.

Steven looked around but found nothing to indicate who the man was. He went back to the door and stuck his head out into the hall. The officer had not returned yet, but Steven knew he would do so soon.

Steven caught the name next to the door. *Mathias Lotta.*

Steven rushed back in. He grabbed a pillow from a chair in the room and slowly approached the bed.

"God, forgive me," he whispered. "I'm doing this for Emily."

He then placed the pillow over the murderer's head. The murderer struggled, but Steven put all his weight on the pillow. The monitors began to beep as he watched the heartbeat flatline.

He suddenly heard voices from the hall.

He dropped the pillow and ran.

He bumped into a man wearing a white coat. "Hey, what're you doing here?" the man demanded.

Steven did not bother stopping. He was already down the hall and through the staircase entrance.

# FIFTY-THREE

"How did you find it?" Jo asked Rhodes.

The moment she received the call, she got there as fast as she could.

Rhodes told her about Simon's tip. "Who's with Mathias?" he asked.

Jo told him about what happened at the hospital.

Rhodes frowned. "I didn't think Chief Baker could do that."

"I didn't either, but he did, and now I don't know what will happen to Mathias."

"He knows something, and he was going to tell us," Rhodes said.

Jo nodded. "They'll probably move him somewhere," she said. "I don't think he'll survive the trip."

"Then, we'll never know why he lured us to the water facility."

Jo did not say anything. She watched as Tarik and Irina dusted the Fiat for fingerprints. She doubted the killer had been careless enough to leave any prints behind. The prints they would find would belong to Emily Bennett and her family.

"We're going to scour the area," Jo said.

"For what?" Rhodes asked.

"To see if Emily is anywhere here."

Rhodes frowned. "I think the killer only wanted to dump the car. I don't think he'd keep his hostage anywhere near it. It would jeopardize his plans."

Jo sighed. "Maybe you're right. But right now, we don't have much to go on except for that car, so we're going to do our due diligence and hope we find something that might lead us to her."

Rhodes watched as she walked away. He could tell she knew it was a futile effort, but she did not want to give up hope. He did not want to either, but as the clock ticked down, he had a sinking feeling they did not have enough time to save Emily.

## FIFTY-FOUR

Steven exited the hospital via a staff-only exit and discarded the white coat. He walked to his car with his head down. The commotion outside had died down, which meant everything was going back to normal.

*It won't be normal, though*, he thought. *I just killed a killer. But I did what others wouldn't, and I saved my wife.*

He knew the authorities would have to make an announcement to the media, and when they did, the killer would have to let his wife go. The killer had given them an ultimatum, and he had fulfilled it. He just hoped the announcement was soon. He could not wait to hold Emily again. She was the love of his life. He only hoped he could keep his emotions in check when he finally saw her. Emily must already be a wreck, and if she saw him crying, she would fall apart even more.

Also, he was not sure if he could ever tell her what he did for her. On the one hand, she would be grateful he had saved her life, but on the other, she would be horrified he had taken another life.

He would deal with that later. At that moment, all he cared about was having his family complete again.

He entered the parking lot and moved past the rows of cars. His brother should be waiting for him by his car. His brother had done his part, and Steven had done his. Together they had gotten the job done.

He spotted his car in the distance and saw his brother waiting for him in the passenger seat. His brother smiled and waved to him. Steven smiled and waved back.

He took two more steps, anticipating the announcement of Mathias's death.

Uniformed officers surrounded him. One of them came up to him and yelled, "Sir, put your hands in the air."

Bennett's shoulders sagged as he raised his hands.

He was cuffed and taken to a room in the hospital. The room had no windows, but there was a table and a chair for him to sit in.

A minute later, a man came in. He was tall and had a scowl over his face. "I'm Chief Baker of the Bridgeton Police Department. Do you know why you are here, Mr. Bennett?"

Steven decided to play it cool. "I'm not sure. Why am I here?"

"Don't play games with us, Mr. Bennett. We have a doctor who saw you come out of a patient's room after you had tried to smother him with a pillow."

"You have no proof," Steven said.

The chief stared at him in disbelief. "We have security footage of you entering the hospital, removing a white lab coat from a linen closet, and proceeding to a patient's room. We also know your brother was the one who instigated the explosion outside the hospital. There are closed-circuit TV cameras all around this place."

Steven's head dropped. The jig was up.

"What the hell were you thinking, Mr. Bennett?" Baker asked.

"I was thinking of saving my wife," Steven replied. "You can put me in jail, I don't care, but you let the media know that the murderer is dead. I want my wife's kidnapper to know the deed is done. He can now let go of my wife."

"You dumb shit," Baker growled, "the person you tried to kill was not Mathias Lotta."

Steven's jaw dropped. "What?"

"We moved Lotta to a secure location. In his place is a fifty-year-old patient who's suffering from liver failure. If it weren't for a doctor's quick intervention, you'd have killed him."

"But… but his name was on the door…" Steven said, dumbfounded.

"The new patient had just been moved into that room not ten minutes before. If you hadn't started all the commotion, the nurses would've already made all the changes."

Steven put his face in his palms. "Oh my god. What have I done?"

The chief crossed his arms over his chest.

"I'm so sorry," Steven said as he began to sob.

# FIFTY-FIVE

Jo returned to the office, feeling like her trip had been a waste. They had searched the area surrounding the Fiat and had come up empty.

*Rhodes was right*, she thought. *The killer was only there to dump the vehicle. He is keeping Emily somewhere else.*

As Jo moved toward her desk, Chris waved her over.

"What is it?" she asked. He was slouched in front of his computer, wearing his headphones. "If it's another Scandinavian rock band you just discovered, I'm not interested."

"No. I think I've got something," he replied, holding the headphones for her.

"What?"

"Just watch."

He played the video of Emily pleading for her life. At the end of it, Jo said, "I've seen it before. What did I miss?"

"I tried focusing on the image, but there is nothing I could see that would point to where she's being held. There are no windows, no photos, no mirrors, nothing to describe the surroundings. It's like she's in a black hole with only a light on her face so that we could identify her."

"I can see that," Jo said, sounding a little impatient. "What's your point?"

"So, instead of focusing on the image, I've tried listening to the sounds instead." He raised the volume and played the video again.

Emily's voice boomed in the headphones. Jo twisted her face. "It's too loud."

"Sorry, I'm going to lower her vocals and isolate the background noise." He clicked and typed and then said, "Listen carefully now. It appears at the end."

Through the headphones, she could still hear Emily's words, albeit very indistinctly, but then there was a distant rumble like someone had blown a horn.

"What is that?" Jo asked, turning to Chris.

"At first, I couldn't tell either, but something about the sound bothered me, particularly how her voice echoed inside the room she's in. No room in a house or even a basement would echo like that. But when I heard that rumble, it confirmed my suspicion."

"And that is?" Jo asked anxiously.

"She is in a shipping container, and that noise is from—"

"A ship horn," Jo finished for him. "She's at the Bridgeton Port!"

# FIFTY-SIX

Chief Baker stared at the comatose body of Mathias Lotta. His face was bloated and his eyes were puffy and shut.

The medications that kept him alive had altered his appearance, but that did not matter to Baker. To him, Mathias still looked like a murderer.

Baker could not believe this man had tortured and killed three people, including one of his detectives. *How was I supposed to stay objective after what this man has done?* he thought. *I swear, there should be a law that lets people like him die. It was not like we'd be killing him, we'd simply not be helping him stay alive. If his body could survive without any assistance, then fine, but if it didn't, well, that's just nature taking its course. This bastard showed Crowder and his other victims no mercy, so why should we?*

Whatever the FBI thought he was hiding was not worth the trouble this man had caused. A husband was now under arrest for trying to save his wife's life. *Do I blame him? Hell no. I would have done the same thing if I was in his shoes.*

This murderer was a thorn in the side of the Bridgeton PD. He was a reminder of what he had done to the department. The pain he had inflicted upon the force was something Baker would not forget. And Crowder's death would forever stain Baker's career because the detective's death had occurred on Baker's watch.

A man entered the room. He was a doctor. "What's going on?" he asked.

"We're moving him," Baker said.

"You can't. He won't survive the move."

"Well, we'll just have to take the chance, won't we?" Baker replied dismissively.

The doctor did not like that answer. "This is not right," he said. "As his physician, I can't let you—"

"Don't worry, doc," Baker interjected. "He's no longer in your care."

"What?"

Gilkin entered the room and said, "We're handing him over to the Bridgeton PD."

"But why?" the doctor asked.

"Do you want to deal with what's happening at the hospital?" Gilkin asked. "Someone just tried to kill one of our patients. I can't have people running around my hospital endangering the lives of my patients and my staff."

"But we are sworn to protect life," the doctor replied. "If you move him now, you'll seriously jeopardize his survival."

"It's not our call anymore. It's the Bridgeton PD's."

The doctor turned to Baker. "Where will you take him?"

The chief said, "There is another hospital—a smaller one—about a hundred miles from here. It's far from major areas and is not well-known. We can better protect him at that location."

"It will take you several hours to get there," the doctor said. "He won't make it through the journey."

"Then it'll depend on how badly he wants to live," Baker said.

# FIFTY-SEVEN

The Jetta raced down the highway. Jo had her flashing red light attached to her roof. Walters was next to her, and she did not protest Jo's speed. There was no time for delays.

Tarik and Irina followed them in Irina's Kia. Tarik's Mercedes had gotten new tires, but back at the office, Irina had looked at him and said, "We are taking *my* car this time."

They entered the Bridgeton Port, and it suddenly dawned on Jo how difficult their task would be. There were rows upon rows of shipping containers. If Emily was in one of them, finding her would not be easy.

Jo spotted a port authority worker. She asked where the port manager was. He pointed further down and said, "His office is on a raised platform. You can't miss it."

Jo drove up and spotted a room the size of a shipping container sitting on what looked like stilts.

The team parked and got out. "Wait here," Jo said to Tarik and Irina.

Jo and Walters went up the metal stairs and found a man with a bushy beard wearing a turtleneck and round glasses inside the room. "We're closed for the night," he said, looking up from his desk. "Come back in the morning."

"We're looking for a shipping container," Jo said, showing her credentials.

The manager sighed. He pointed out the window. "Which one?"

Jo realized why the manager's office was high up. She could see the entire port from her vantage point. There were more shipping containers than she thought. They were stacked on top of each other, some stacks as high as ten containers.

Jo felt a stab of pain in her chest. She gritted her teeth and waited for it to pass. Walters was behind her, so she did not see Jo's reaction.

Jo knew why the pain had reappeared. The stress of their task was monumental.

"I've got thousands of containers," the manager said. "Which one are you looking for?"

Jo had no idea. All she knew was that one of them was holding Emily Bennett.

"What about any shipments that came in last night?" Jo asked. Emily had disappeared twenty-four hours ago, so that would narrow their search.

He adjusted his glasses and checked his computer. "We had three shipments come in yesterday."

"Okay, how many containers?"

He kept staring at his monitor. "Over three hundred and fifty," he replied.

"What about empty containers?" Jo asked. The killer must have brought Emily in the middle of the night, found a vacant container, and left her inside it.

The manager pointed to an area away from the port. "Over there. It's easier for the trucks to load them there."

Walters said, "Then we search there."

Jo shook her head. "In the video, we were able to hear the noise of a ship horn. This means the container has to be closer to the water, not away from it."

"Then where do we look?" Walters asked.
Jo had no idea.

## FIFTY-EIGHT

Everything was set.

Two police cruisers, along with an ambulance, would leave the hospital from the main exit. As expected, the crowd and the media would follow them. But this was only a diversion. A lone ambulance would then leave from the back of the hospital and take the suspect to a location far away.

Chief Baker could not help but smile. He had come up with the plan, and he had no doubt it would work. In one single act, he would be able to get rid of both the mob outside the hospital and Mathias Lotta.

He was certain Lotta would not survive the long journey. The staff at the other hospital would not receive a patient but a dead body.

Lotta's survival was of no concern to him. The safety of the people in the hospital was.

Sure, he would get some heat for Lotta's death, but it would only be for a short period. The media would quickly become preoccupied with the next major crisis or event, and Mathias Lotta would be forgotten. When all was said and done, he might even receive a medal for his actions. It might not be right away, but when people realized the decision he made was right, they would want to bestow some honor upon him.

Plus, when news spread of Mathias's death, the killer would be hard-pressed to let Emily Bennett go. If he did not, well, his next threat would fall on deaf ears. In fact, the governor had assured him if anything happened to Emily, he would throw his full support behind finding the killer, and Baker would be at the forefront of the search.

"Is he ready?" Baker asked, turning to Gilkin.

"We're prepping the patient now," she said.

"Once he's loaded into the ambulance, you make the announcement. Everyone will see the convoy leaving and assume he is being moved via the front of the hospital. Some will try to impede or delay the journey, but by then, the other ambulance will be long gone. If they ask you where they are taking him, you tell them the truth. You don't know because we didn't tell you. If they ask you why you tell them it was for the safety of the staff and patients."

Gilkin was silent for a moment. She then said, "He might not make it, you know."

Baker could sense she was having second thoughts. "Just remember, he's a serial killer," he said. "He's also responsible for what's going on out there." The chants outside were continuing without letup. "You do not want any more situations in your hospital."

She sighed. "Anything to end this madness."

## FIFTY-NINE

From where she was standing, Jo could see the sun rising over the horizon. Emily's time was slipping through her hands like grains of sand.

Tarik and Irina appeared by the door.

"We're running out of time," Tarik said.

Jo did not reply. She just stared out the window.

Walters said, "We don't know where she could be."

"We can check all the containers," Irina suggested.

Walters pointed. "Take a look for yourself."

When Irina and Tarik did, they realized what they were up against. Emily could be in any one of them.

"We have to start the search," Tarik said. "Even if we're late, we have to find her body."

"Maybe the killer might not go through with it," Irina suggested.

"I doubt that," Tarik said. "If he does not follow through with his threat, nobody will take him seriously. We have to do something."

Jo closed her eyes and tried to think. "We need more information," she said. She pulled out her cell phone and dialed a number. "Chris, we are at the port, but we don't know where Emily is. In the video, did you see anything else?"

"Like what?"

"Anything in the background, maybe."

"It was dark."

"Can you check again?" she asked.

She heard him typing on his computer, followed by the sound of the video.

Chris came back on. "I think I might have something."

"What?"

"It's right at the end, around the same time we heard the ship's horn. After the victim ends her statement, she drops her head to cry. It was only for a second or two, but I saw boxes stacked up behind her, and on one of them, I can spot the letters M, A, U, R. The video then cuts off."

"Thanks, Chris," Jo said, hanging up.

She turned to the port manager. "Does M, A, U, R mean anything to you?"

He shrugged. "I don't know, should it?"

"It could be a clue to finding our hostage."

The manager was befuddled. "It could be the name of a shipping company."

"No, it's not," Tarik said.

They turned to him.

"I think M, A, U, R, are partial letters for a country. Mauritius."

"What?" Jo asked.

"Mauritius is an island in the Indian Ocean," Tarik replied.

Jo turned to the port manager. "Yesterday or the day before, did you get any shipments from Mauritius?"

He quickly checked his computer and said, "As a matter of fact, we did."

"Where are they?"

"I'll show you."

They followed him down the stairs and headed for the other side of the port.

The sun was now fully visible.

Jo prayed they were not too late.

They moved past rows of containers until they came to a stop. The manager pointed at a stack. "Those eight containers all came from Mauritius last night."

Jo rushed over and spotted the container in question right away. "I think this lock's been tampered with."

Tarik pulled out his weapon, reversed his grip to the barrel, and used the grip to crack the lock in half.

The rest of the team pulled out their weapons in case they faced something unexpected. Tarik and Irina grabbed the door handles, and when Jo gave the signal, they swung them open.

Jo aimed the light and entered.

It did not take long for her to spot Emily. She was in the middle of the container. Her arms and legs were tied to a chair, and her head was slumped down to her chest.

There was a camera in front of her.

Jo rushed over and checked Emily's pulse.

"Get the paramedics," Jo said. "She's alive."

## SIXTY

Chief Baker checked his watch for the umpteenth time.

*What is taking so long?* he wondered. *They should've been on the road by now.* Every minute Mathias Lotta was in the hospital, the chances of something bad happening increased.

The crowd outside the hospital had become rowdy. News had spread of Steven Bennett's arrest. Some were appalled by what he had tried to do. Others blamed the FBI and the police for not doing their jobs. Had they ended a murderer's life, Bennett would not have taken the drastic step that he did.

"How long does it take to prep a patient?" Baker asked Gilkin.

She frowned. "It all depends on the condition of the patient and how complicated his situation is."

"Well, I don't really care whether he lives or dies, I just want him out of here," Baker snapped.

Gilkin stared at him.

Baker cleared his throat. "I mean, we need to speed the process up or else we might have another attack in the hospital."

"I'll go check," she said.

A doctor entered the room. He looked pale.

"What's wrong?" Gilkin asked.

"We've got a problem."

"What?"

"You have to come and see."

They hurried down the hall, went up the stairs, and moved past security at the critical care unit.

There was a crowd gathered outside the room when Baker and Gilkin entered it.

Immediately, Baker had a feeling something was not right. None of the monitors were beeping.

Mathias Lotta's eyes were closed, but he did not look any different than the last time Baker had seen him.

Baker turned to a doctor and asked, "What happened?"

The doctor swallowed. "He's dead."

"What?" Baker and Gilkin asked in unison.

The doctor nodded.

"How?" Gilkin asked.

"We don't know," the doctor replied.

"I thought you were prepping him for the move?" Baker asked.

The doctor sighed. "We were. His vitals were stable when I last checked on him."

Baker turned to the officer stationed at the door. "What happened?"

"I… I don't know. As instructed, I only let the staff in and out of the room."

"Who was the last person in the room?" Baker asked.

"A nurse."

"What did she look like?" Gilkin said.

The officer's brow furrowed. "She was short, heavy, and she had brown hair tied into pigtails."

"That's Susan Bayliss," the doctor said.

"Where is she now?" Baker demanded.

They went out to the nurses' station. "Was Susan here today?" Gilkin asked the head nurse.

The head nurse was confused. "Today is Susan's day off," she replied.

Baker said, "One of my officers just saw her right now."

"I don't know what to tell you, but Susan's not scheduled to be in today. Look at our calendar." She pointed to a whiteboard with the names of the doctors and nurses on duty. Bayliss's name was not on it.

Baker quickly pulled out his cell phone. He provided the name and description of the suspect to his officers. He hung up and said, "If she's still in the building, we'll find her."

They returned to the room, where the doctor had placed a white sheet over Lotta's body. "I'll have to conduct an autopsy. Without it, I can't say for certain what the cause of death was."

"Damn," Baker grumbled.

Gilkin's eyes filled with confusion. "I thought you didn't care if he lived or died?"

"I don't, but I didn't want it to happen here, not now, not under my supervision," he huffed. "The FBI is going to have a field day with this."

His phone rang. He listened and hung up. "They just found Bayliss leaving via the emergency exit."

## SIXTY-ONE

She sat across from them with a look of defiance on her face. She was dressed in scrubs, but she also wore a light sweater to combat the cool breeze outside.

They were in a room not far from where Mathias's dead body now lay. Chief Baker stared at Susan Bayliss while Gilkin was eerily silent as if someone had sucked the life out of her.

Baker almost felt sorry for Gilkin. The woman had done everything right. She had acted upon his advice and was preparing to move Lotta, but then one of her employees had decided to go rogue and take matters into her own hands.

Baker knew the hospital board would come down hard on Gilkin. He had seen similar things happen in his own line of work. They would want a scapegoat, and she would be the one. That was unfair on so many levels. If the supervisor knew what the employee was up to, would they not have prevented anything from happening in the first place? But the media and the public would not care. They wanted the satisfaction in knowing someone had been disciplined, regardless of whether they deserved it or not.

Baker said, "Ms. Bayliss, why did you do it?"

"It's *Mrs.* Bayliss," she replied. "I'm married."

"All right. Mrs. Bayliss, why did you commit murder?"

"I couldn't stop thinking about Emily Bennett. I have two kids the same age as hers. When I saw Mr. Bennett on the news pleading for his wife's safe return, my heart broke. *What if that was me?* I thought. What if my husband was on the news begging for my safety? What would my kids be going through knowing I was in harm's way? What would happen to them after I was gone?" She looked at Baker. "Those thoughts tore away at me. I wanted to do something. I wanted to help. I would have volunteered to help search for Emily, but then I realized Mathias Lotta was in my hospital, in my department. It was then that I realized God had given me an opportunity to do some good."

"You murdered another person," Baker said.

"He was already dying," she said with a scowl. "His chance of survival was twenty percent at best. I would know because on a number of occasions, I had cared for him. Plus, he was a cold-blooded killer. He killed all those people…"

She shuddered at the thought.

"You're a nurse. Your duty is to preserve life."

"I'm also a wife and a mother. I wanted to preserve another person's life who also happens to be a wife and a mother."

"What did you do to him?" Baker asked.

"I injected him with a concoction of beta-blockers. They slowed his heart until it stopped beating."

Baker looked over at Gilkin, hoping she had questions of her own.

She was staring at the table, probably lost in thought about how her career had gone down the drain.

There was a knock at the door, and an officer came in. "Sir, there is an important message for you."

"What is it?" Baker asked, annoyed.

The officer glanced at Susan and then said, "We just received a call from the FBI. They have located Emily Bennett. She is alive and safe."

Baker turned to Susan. "If you had let us do our job, you probably wouldn't be facing a charge of first-degree murder."

Susan's hands began to tremble as her defiant look crumbled.

Baker got up and left the room. He was in no mood to see her break down once she realized what a big mistake she had made.

## SIXTY-TWO

Jo decided to head home. It had been an exhausting day. With the adrenaline worn off, she was suddenly feeling fatigued. The pain in her chest had reappeared, and she realized her heart had overworked itself.

Emily was taken to the nearest hospital for a thorough checkup, but there was nothing that indicated she had been harmed. Physically, she was fine. Mentally, though, she would have to live with her ordeal for the rest of her life.

Jo did manage to spend a few minutes with her before the paramedics took her away. The night she was kidnapped, Emily was in the parking lot of a grocery store. She was putting groceries in the back of her car when she felt a sharp pain in her neck. She grabbed at her neck and found a syringe stuck in her. Before she could turn and see who had done it, she felt light-headed and dizzy. Her knees buckled and she was sure she would drop to the pavement. Instead, someone grabbed her and lifted her up in the air. She could not see who it was, only that the perpetrator wore a blue overcoat. She was placed on the floor of a vehicle. She remembered the feel of the carpet on her face. It could have been a cargo van. There were no windows. She then blacked out. When she came to, she was inside a dark metal room.

Jo had more questions for Emily, but when she broke down, recounting her nightmare, Jo decided to let her go. She had suffered enough. The initial shock of the kidnapping had not worn off.

Jo was relieved that Emily was safe, but she could not help but feel the killer had won. Right after they had found Emily, Walters received the call from Chief Baker. To say that Walters was not pleased with what she heard would be an understatement. Walters was already on her way to the hospital, and Jo was certain she would give the chief a piece of her mind. Jo did not want to be there when she did.

It did not matter who was right and who was wrong. What mattered was that Mathias was dead, and the killer was still out there.

Jo was not sure how she truly felt now that Mathias was gone. A part of her wanted to see him go the same way as his victims. Another part of her, however, wanted to see him live and serve time for his crimes.

In a strange way, though, the weight had been lifted from her shoulders. She was no longer burdened by the secret he was holding. Even if he had not died now, how long could she have waited for him to come out of his coma?

It was better that he was gone. Now she and the rest of Bridgeton could move on.

Jo spotted her house in the distance. She needed a well-deserved rest. If Dr. Cohen found out she was back on the job, he would rule her unfit for duty. She could not risk that happening. She only went back because a life was at stake.

She would take the next two weeks off. This is what she had told Walters at the port, and that was what she was going to do.

She approached her driveway and felt a sudden impulse.

She swung the Jetta around, realizing there was someplace else she needed to be.

## SIXTY-THREE

Sully and Patti were married under a makeshift tent behind Sully's trailer home. It looked like the entire neighborhood had shown up for their wedding. There were bikers, truckers, hillbillies, and people who had nothing better to do.

Rhodes was dressed in the suit his father had given him. The suit was a bit loose, but Rhodes did not care, just as long as he did not have to wear it again.

Sully had worn a rented tuxedo while his bride had worn a white dress that she had bought at a second-hand shop. The dress might have been elegant once, but after what Patti did to the outfit, it was something entirely different. The length of the skirt had been cut so that Patti's legs could be seen, the sleeves were removed in order to expose her toned arms, and the neckline was lowered so that Patti's cleavage could be visible.

The priest who presided over the wedding was a hippie. Rhodes had seen him smoking a joint prior to the ceremony.

Rhodes was not surprised by any of this. In fact, he half-expected it. This was, after all, the wedding of Sullivan Rhodes, a well-known thief and conman.

The entire ceremony lasted half an hour, which was quickly followed by the reception.

Rhodes walked up to the makeshift minibar, though it was not really a minibar per se. It was a man with a beer cooler selling drinks to the guests. What else did he expect from his father? Sully did not like paying for anything if he did not have to. At least there were cold sandwiches and a cake for dessert. *That should mean something*, Rhodes thought.

Rhodes sat on a plastic chair and sipped his bottle of beer.

Sully came over and sat next to him. "So, what'd you think of the wedding, son?"

Rhodes shrugged. "Nice, I guess."

Sully grinned. "What'd you think of Patti? Did she look hot or what?"

"I think all the men were staring at her."

Sully's grin widened. "They were, weren't they?"

Rhodes took another sip of his beer. He hated small talk in general, and there was no way he wanted to indulge in some with his father.

"Where do you plan on going for your honeymoon?" Rhodes asked, not really caring for the answer.

Sully leaned over and smiled. "I'm glad you asked. As my best man, I was thinking you could gift your old man some cash so he could take his new bride out on the town. What do you think?"

*And there it is*, Rhodes thought. *Sully always has an angle. He didn't make me his best man because I'm his son, he just wanted a loan.*

Rhodes finished his drink and stood up. "You already got your gift."

"I did?" Sully asked, surprised.

"Yep. If I didn't lie for you, you'd probably be in jail right now for robbing that bank. Enjoy your wedding, Sully."

Rhodes walked away.

## SIXTY-FOUR

Jo was at her mother's care facility. She stood outside her mother's room, but she did not go in. The woman sitting in front of the TV was frail, but she had no strands of gray in her hair. It had been dyed, something Jo had made sure the staff did every two weeks. She was dressed in a white gown, and her nails were painted red. She had on matching lipstick, but her mouth barely moved.

Elaine Pullinger was once Miss Wyoming. She was a stunner in her youth, and all the boys had doted on her. She could have had any man she wanted. A lawyer, a businessman, even a doctor, had proposed to her. But she married an FBI agent.

Jo could see why her father had gone after her. What she still did not understand was why he ended up breaking her heart. No matter what Walters told her, Jo could not condone her father's actions. No amount of stress or pressure could justify infidelity.

Her mother loved her father even more than her father loved her. It was why she had fallen apart after discovering the affair.

A woman came up to Jo. "Hey there, nice to have you back," she said.

It was Jackie, her mother's primary caretaker.

"How's she doing?" Jo asked.

"She has her good days and then she has her bad," Jackie replied. "Today is one of the better days, so it's good that you dropped by. Go in. Spend time with her. She'll be happy to see you."

Jo doubted that. Her mother barely acknowledged that Jo was even there, but it was not that she did not want to see her daughter. Her mind was in a place far from reality.

Jo entered the room and spotted Walters's latest vase of tulips in the corner. A part of her wanted to remove them, but another part knew they comforted her mother. The flowers were also Walters's way of asking for forgiveness, and Jo had no right to deny her mother the opportunity to accept or reject Walters's gesture.

Jo pulled up a chair next to her. The TV was playing a soap opera. Her mother loved watching them when Jo was young. Jackie made sure she got to see an episode each day.

Her mother stared at the screen. She gave no indication that she was aware Jo was in the room.

Jo was used to her mother's behavior after so many years. Whether her mom knew she had visited or not was beside the point. What was important was that Jo had made an effort to come.

Jo put her hand over hers. "Mom, I didn't know that dad had hurt you so much. I didn't know that he had been unfaithful to you. I didn't know why you were suffering when it happened. I understand now why you couldn't tell me. Because it would've broken my heart. I'm sorry I wasn't there for you more. I promise I will be now. I love you, mom."

Jo had tears in her eyes.

For a brief moment, nothing happened. Her mother continued staring at the TV.

Jo wiped her eyes.

She felt her mother's grip tighten on her hand. She looked up.

There were tears in her mother's eyes.

Jo put her arms around her mom and hugged her.

## SIXTY-FIVE

Rhodes sat on his sofa, watching the news. He had already found out that the FBI was able to locate Emily Bennett. He also found out that Mathias Lotta had died. The news reporter did not share how he had succumbed, but Rhodes had a feeling it was not from natural causes. Something had happened. Maybe the hospital had yielded to the public's demands. They would never admit it, but Rhodes felt otherwise. He found it odd that Mathias was alive for the past three months, but when the Emily Bennett situation arose, he was suddenly dead. He did not think it was a coincidence.

There was a knock at the door. Rhodes was not surprised. He was expecting company.

He opened the door and said, "Come in, Mac."

Mac came in holding a box.

"What's that?" Rhodes asked.

"I'll tell you later. But first, I'm sure you're interested to know what happened to my investigation."

"I'm assuming you charged Adam Channing for the murders of Jenny and Myron Goldsmith."

Mac raised an eyebrow. "Yes, but how?"

Rhodes waited for Mac to answer his own question.

"You were right when you said Adam was in two places on the night the Goldsmiths' were murdered. Although the footage did show him and his friend entering the concert, we were unable to verify the individual who left the concert in the middle and then returned right before it ended. We did find out that Adam's friend had purchased not two but three tickets, which would further confirm your theory that Adam had used the extra ticket to re-enter the show. But it was still not enough to convict him. There were witnesses who saw Adam arrive at the concert around the time of the murders. They also saw him leave. I don't believe he was drunk at the end of the concert when he became loud and belligerent. It was a façade. He wanted security to see and remember him. He knew they would be his perfect alibi when the police eventually came knocking on his door. But even with everything we had, it was still not enough to charge him."

Rhodes was intrigued. "So, how did you connect him to the murders?"

Mac smiled. "His friend. You asked me to check for any convenience stores or gas stations near the Goldsmiths' residence. I did, and I found a convenience store about a block away from their house. I checked the security footage and found that a white Ford Taurus had passed the store twice. The first time it was going towards the Goldsmiths' residence, and the second time it was driving away. The time-stamped on the footage matched the coroner's report of when the Goldsmiths' had been killed. The Taurus had passed too fast for us to capture the license plate, but it was still enough for us to go after the friend."

"Then what happened?" Rhodes asked.

"We brought him in for questioning. We told him we had footage of his vehicle near the Goldsmiths' residence at the time of their murder. When we pressured him to tell us the truth or else we'd charge him with double homicide, he broke down and confessed. He told us it was Adam who had borrowed his car to go and commit the murders. Adam was also the one who had come up with the plan. Naturally, we wanted proof that it was not the friend but Adam, who was responsible for the crime. The friend didn't know where the murder weapon was. Adam had told him he had disposed of the weapon. The friend did, however, have Adam's clothes at his apartment: the jacket and baseball cap he'd worn to disguise himself when he left in the middle of the concert. He also found for us Adam's sneakers in the garbage bin. Luckily for us, the soles contained blood splatters. We matched them to Jenny and Myron Goldsmith. It's not surprising how quickly people will turn on someone when their freedom is on the line. Adam is now looking at life behind bars. And this is all thanks to you, Martin."

Rhodes shrugged. "You did all the heavy lifting. I just pointed you in the right direction."

"I have something for you," Mac said. He placed the box on the dining table.

"What's in it?" Rhodes asked.

"I found it in the precinct's evidence locker."

Rhodes walked over and opened the box. Inside he saw a framed picture of himself and his now-ex-wife. There was a baseball he had caught at a major league game, a plaque he had received for outstanding police work, and other items from his desk at the Newport PD. He had not had time to retrieve his belongings. He was already in police custody for murder. He always thought the department had either returned his stuff to his ex-wife or had disposed of it. Even if they had kept his mementos, there was no way he would go back to his old job to retrieve them.

"Thank you, Mac," Rhodes said.

"I figured you might want them."

A part of him did, but another part of him did not. They were a reminder of who he was before his life turned upside down.

"I appreciate you bringing them for me," Rhodes said. He could not throw everything away. He valued some of the keepsakes.

"I also brought something else," Mac said.

He stuck his hand in his jacket pocket and pulled out a shiny object. He held it up. Rhodes recognized the object the moment he saw it. It was his detective badge. "Unfortunately, you can't keep it. It would be against the law. But I knew you'd want to see it one more time."

Rhodes took his badge. It felt heavy in his hands. He moved his fingers over the numbers. Even then, he still remembered his badge number.

"Thanks, Mac," Rhodes said. His eyes were moist.

Mac smiled. "Hold on to it for now. I'm not leaving right away. Do you mind if I grab a beer from your fridge?"

Rhodes nodded, but his eyes remained fixed on his badge.

## SIXTY-SIX

Jo knocked on the door and waited.

"Hey Jo," her sister-in-law said as she opened the door.

"Hi Kim."

"Come on in."

Kim waved her inside.

"Where's Chrissy?" Jo asked.

"She's at a sleepover party at her friend's house."

"That smells good," Jo said. Her mouth was watering.

"I'm making chili stew with brown rice."

"You don't mind if I join you?"

Kim looked at her. "Why would you say that? You know you're always welcome at our house."

"Sam probably told you about my meeting with him."

"He did."

"I'm sorry for putting my foot in your and Sam's business," Jo said. "I love you guys so much, and I only wanted to help."

"I can't say I was happy when I found out, but I'm glad you did it."

"You are?" Jo was surprised.

"Yes. It got Sam and me talking again, and we realized things may not be good between us right now, but it doesn't mean we should throw away everything we've worked so hard for. We do care about each other, and we have a daughter we adore. We're willing to work through our differences and give our marriage a chance."

Jo choked up. "You won't believe how happy I am to hear that."

Kim said, "Come here. Give me a hug."

"Where is Sam?" Jo asked.

"He's in the garage. I think you better go talk to him."

Jo found Sam working on a lawnmower.

"Hey," she said.

"Hey," he replied.

"What's wrong with it?" Jo asked.

Sam looked at the mower. "It won't start for the most part, and when it does, it stops abruptly."

"You want me to take a look?" Jo asked. She was always good with tools and machinery, which was why she got along better with their father. Sam was more like their mother. He was organized and was on top of everything that was happening in the house, but he was helpless when it came to mechanical things.

"Be my guest," Sam said.

Jo checked the mower and said, "The spark plug needs to be changed. You got a spare one?"

Sam went over to his toolbox and returned with a brand new spark plug.

Jo replaced the plug and pulled the starter rope. The mower coughed and then came to life.

"Wow, thanks," Sam said.

Jo smiled and shut the mower down.

There was silence between them before Sam said, "You okay? I mean, what I told you about Dad?"

"I wasn't before, but now I am."

He nodded.

"You were always okay with it?" she asked.

Sam shrugged. "At first, I was livid. How could he do that to mom? But then, as I got older, I realized people are not perfect. Hell, I'm not perfect."

Jo smirked. "That I agree with one hundred percent."

"Thanks for the vote of confidence." He smiled. "Dad made a bad decision, and he could have hid it from mom, but he didn't. He just didn't realize how devastated she would be. I'm sorry I never told you, Jo. I knew how much you wanted to be like Dad, and I didn't want to destroy that."

"I know."

"So, how's your vacation going?" he asked.

Jo rolled her eyes. "You won't believe what happened."

"Well, you can tell me all about it at dinner."

## SIXTY-SEVEN

After Mac left, Rhodes felt restless. Maybe it had something to do with the stuff Mac brought from his old precinct. The mementos had triggered a flood of memories from his detective days, especially his badge, which he never thought he would see or touch again.

The badge had meant a great deal to him. It defined who he was. He was proud of carrying his badge, and he never took for granted the power it gave him. Doors opened whenever he flashed his badge, and people talked freely once they saw the shield stamped *Detective, N.P.D.* Now he felt naked without it. He had to beg, plead, and cajole information out of people. Intimidation worked only against certain types of people, like Yevgeny. Those who knew the law knew he could do nothing to them.

He left his apartment and decided to go for a drive. He did not want to be stuck in a cramped space surrounded by his thoughts.

There was also something he wanted to check out, an item he had heard about on the news. Emily Bennett had mentioned she may have been taken in a cargo van. She was not sure. She was drugged at the time. She remembered being placed on the floor of a vehicle.

Emily's mention of a van made Rhodes uneasy.

He drove back to where Simon had heard the gunshot. He was not sure what he would find, but he remembered seeing something the last time he was here.

He drove past several parked vehicles and spotted a van parked next to a 4x4.

He got out. There were a couple of parking tickets on the windshield. He scanned them. They were from the past two days.

*Wasn't it two nights ago that Emily was kidnapped?* he thought.

He got closer to the driver's side window and scanned the van's interior. He found nothing out of the ordinary. He went around and did the same from the back window.

He noticed something on the floor of the van. He could not tell what it was. There were no windows on either side, so lighting was poor. He cupped his eyes and leaned closer to the window.

He finally made out what he was seeing.

A pale hand was visible.

He pulled the door handle. To his surprise, the back door was unlocked.

He swung the door open and saw that the hand belonged to a man. His eyes were closed, but there was blood on the side of his head.

There was also a gun in his right hand.

Rhodes shut the door and returned to his Malibu. There was a pay phone he had spotted a block from where he was.

He had to make a call.

## SIXTY-EIGHT

Within twenty minutes, the FBI was all over the cargo van.

Rhodes had called Jo, but she was not picking up, so he called the Bridgeton FBI office.

Walters was the first one on the scene. She was not pleased to see Rhodes. "What were you doing here?" she asked.

"Where is Agent Pullinger?" Rhodes asked, instead.

"She's on leave."

Rhodes was surprised by her response. Jo was a dedicated agent, and he knew she would not miss this unless her leave was involuntary. Rhodes was aware of Jo's heart condition. He had stumbled upon it during the Train Killings. He had saved her from an oncoming train after she had been attacked in the subway tunnel.

He hoped her leave had nothing to do with her heart.

"You didn't answer my question," Walters said. "What were you doing here?"

Rhodes knew the cold response he would get if Jo was not there. He had debated calling the Bridgeton PD, but there was still some animosity toward him after he had solved a case that once belonged to the deceased Detective Jay Crowder.

Rhodes said, "I was here before when we found the Fiat…"

"And now you found the cargo van. What a coincidence," Walters said.

255

She was baiting him, but he was not going to bite. "I remember seeing a cargo van the last time I was here, and when I heard on the news that Emily Bennett was also taken in a cargo van, I knew it was worth checking out."

"And when you did, you happened to find a dead body. How convenient," Walters replied.

Rhodes was about to open his mouth when Tarik came over.

"You might find this interesting," he said.

"What?" Walters asked.

"The van belongs to a Gary Finkelstein."

"Why is that important?" Walters replied, annoyed that Tarik had interrupted her questioning of Rhodes.

Tarik said, "Five years ago, Finkelstein and Emily Bennett worked for the same company, but during that time, Emily filed a harassment suit against Finkelstein, citing abuse of power, intimidation, and threat of dismissal. Finkelstein was her boss. Finkelstein lost the case and was fired. He has been unemployed ever since. Also, Emily mentioned her assailant was wearing a blue overcoat. Finkelstein is wearing one right now."

Walters turned to the van. "So, when Finkelstein found out Emily had been freed, he realized she would describe him to the police, so he decided to take his own life.

"That would explain the single gunshot wound to the head and the gun on his person," Tarik said.

Walters said, "This had nothing to do with Mathias Lotta, or even George Moll or Kyle Summers, for that matter. This was always about getting revenge against Emily Bennett."

"Looks like it," Tarik said.

They were wrong, Rhodes knew. The real killer had shot Finkelstein in the van and then had driven Emily's car to another location. It was why Simon had heard a gunshot and then seen the Fiat drive away.

Rhodes wanted to tell Walters this, but he held his tongue. *Let them investigate it further*, he thought. *Sooner or later, they'll find out the truth.*

He began to walk away.

"I'm not done asking you questions," Walters said.

"I'm done answering your questions," Rhodes replied. "If you think I'm responsible or had anything to do with this, then you can arrest me. Otherwise, I'm going home."

Neither Tarik nor Walters were going to arrest the man who had found Emily Bennett's kidnapper.

It would be bad publicity.

## SIXTY-NINE

Jo was at home. She had heard her cell phone ring several times, but she did not answer it. It was probably someone asking about her relationship with Mathias. She was in no mood to provide an explanation to anyone. It was none of their business.

She was not concerned if any of the calls were from work. Walters was adamant that she take some time off, so she would not be contacting Jo anyway.

She walked around the living room and stared at the Bridgeton Ripper items on the walls. She no longer had any desire to investigate the case. Her obsession was only due to the fact that she blamed the Ripper for her mother's current mental state. She always thought if the Ripper had not killed her father, her parents would still be together and they would have still been a family. Now she knew that was a lie. Her parents were on the road to divorce when her father was killed.

She removed each item from the wall, and after scanning them, she placed them in the garbage bin. It felt good, almost cathartic, to shed herself of this burden. The Bridgeton Ripper was her father's case, not hers. If he had eluded capture for this long, who was to say he would be caught any time soon? She had already devoted too many years of her life to the case. And what if the Ripper had died long ago? Then her search would have been not only futile but also foolish.

Jo pulled down a newspaper article on Annabelle Burton. She was Mathias Lotta's mother, and she was believed to be the Ripper's last victim. Jo knew that was not true. Tara Millwood was killed eighteen years ago. The way she was murdered was similar to the other Ripper victims. There was no proof linking her case to the Ripper's, but Jo believed otherwise.

*It doesn't matter now, though*, she thought. *It's time to get rid of this stuff and move on.*

She was about to place the article in the garbage bin when she stopped. In the article, Annabelle's husband, Ansel—a medical student at that time—stated he was at school when his wife had disappeared. The police later found Lotta's car on the side of the road with his young son sleeping inside, but no sign of his wife. A few hours after that, they found her mutilated body underneath a bridge.

Jo closed her eyes.

During Walters's interview with Dr. Lotta, Walters had asked him about his whereabouts on the night of his wife's disappearance.

She shut her eyes even tighter. She could hear his voice in her head: *I was at home with my son.*

She read the article again. It did not make sense.

She searched and found more articles on Annabelle Burton. Lotta had said the same thing in each of them. He was at school when his wife had disappeared. Then why did he tell Walters he was at home with his son?

Jo grabbed her jacket and left the house.

## SEVENTY

Jo rang the doorbell and waited.

A minute later, Ansel Lotta answered the door.

"Agent Pullinger, is this about my son?" he asked.

Jo stopped. She had forgotten about Mathias's death. Lotta must have heard it on the news like everyone else. *I should have contacted him when I found out,* she thought. *He deserved to know from the agent who had denied him access to his son.*

"I'm sorry about what happened to Mathias," Jo said.

"I'm sure you are," he said dismissively. "I'm going to file a formal complaint with the Bureau. I never got to see him before he died."

"Even if you saw him, he wouldn't have known you were even there," Jo said.

Lotta scowled. "Are you here to tell me I can *now* see his dead body?"

"No. Mathias is no longer in the custody of the FBI. You'll have to contact the Bridgeton PD and arrange it with them."

"Then why are you here?" he asked.

"I have a few questions for you."

"What type of questions?" he replied. "I'm running late for something important."

"It won't take long. It's about the Bridgeton Ripper."

Lotta's eyes narrowed. "Come inside. You can ask me your questions while I get ready."

Jo stood in the spacious hallway while Lotta went into his office. "What did you want to ask me?" he asked from the other room.

"It's about your meeting with my boss."

"What about it?"

"You said on the night your wife disappeared, you were at home with your son."

"Yes, that's correct."

"But I found articles where you stated to the police that on the night your wife had disappeared, you were at school. The police later found your vehicle abandoned by the side of the road with your son sleeping inside. He was all alone."

Lotta came out of his office. "That is what happened."

"Then why did you say something different to Agent Walters?"

He looked confused. "I'm not sure why. What I had told the police is exactly what happened. You have to realize my wife disappeared when my son was still a toddler. A lot has happened since then. Also, it was a traumatic period in my life, and I've tried to forget it. So in my haste, I may have misspoken to your supervisor. Did I break the law?"

Jo shook her head. "No, of course not."

He went back to his office.

Jo said, "Dr. Lotta, in the police reports, it stated that it was *you* who had contacted them about your wife's disappearance. That's what triggered the search for her, and it's how they found your abandoned vehicle."

"If that's what the police report states, then I must have contacted them."

"But you were at school, so how did you know she was missing?" Jo asked.

There was silence. He came out into the hallway. In his left hand was a medical bag, and a stethoscope was in his right.

He frowned. "You are asking me about something that happened twenty years ago."

"I'm sorry about this."

His face creased. "Hmmm… if I remember correctly, my wife used to pick me up after my lab sessions. I was a medical student at that time, you know."

"I'm aware of that," Jo said.

"On that night, I waited for her for over two hours. We didn't have cell phones back then, so I couldn't contact her. I took the bus home, and when I saw she wasn't there, I knew something bad must have happened, so I quickly contacted the police."

*That makes sense*, Jo thought. She looked around. "Where is your family?"

"After all the stuff on the news about Mathias and the lady who was taken hostage, I sent my wife and daughters to my in-laws," he replied.

"That was a good idea," she said.

Dr. Lotta checked his watch. "Sorry, I'm in a rush." He disappeared into his office again.

She scanned the interior of the house. It was elegant and luxurious. "You're heading to your clinic?" she asked, realizing she had no more questions for him.

"I'm actually heading straight to the hospital," he said.

*It is time for me to go*, she thought. She had already wasted too much time here. "The hospital?" she asked, not knowing what else to say.

"Yes, I have a surgery to perform."

Something flashed in her mind, like an explosion, as if her brain was pulling everything together.

*Why didn't I see it before? It was always right in front of me.*

*Maybe I could not because I was always looking in the wrong direction.*

She blinked and then shut her eyes. *The police reports indicated that the Bridgeton Ripper's victims were cut up and then stitched back together. Their organs had been removed and then placed back inside their bodies. This required extreme precision as if the Ripper was performing surgical procedures.*

Jo's eyes moved inside her eyelids.

*It was believed the Ripper was highly educated and was perhaps even in the medical profession.*

Her lips curled into a frown.

*Mathias's mother was a victim of the Ripper. Mathias had always stated his father was a murderer. His father had sent him to a mental institute, and when Mathias got out, he returned to Bridgeton to kill his father.*

Her face contorted.

*Mathias had wanted to tell me something the night he was shot: his father was the Bridgeton Ripper!*

She opened her eyes and found Lotta staring at her.

"Are you okay?" he asked.

She reached for her weapon but realized she was not on duty and had left it at home. Instead, she pulled out her cell phone.

"I have to go," she said.

"You're satisfied with my answers?" he asked.

"Yes… they were quite informative."

She moved toward the front door.

"Let me get that for you," he said from behind her.

"No, I'm fine."

She felt something pinch her neck. She grabbed the object and pulled it out. It was a syringe. She turned and looked over at Lotta. He was staring at her stone-faced.

She tried to reach for the door handle, but her knees buckled. Her hand hit an object on the entry table, and it hit the floor at the same time she did.

Her head spun and her eyes became blurry.

The last image she saw was of Lotta standing over her.

# SEVENTY-ONE

Rhodes stood outside Jo's house and waited. He had already called her several times, but she was not answering her phone.

He wanted to speak to her about the body found in the cargo van. The FBI believed it was a straightforward kidnapping/suicide. Gary Finkelstein kidnapped Emily Bennett because of what happened five years ago, and when she was rescued, he shot and killed himself.

*Highly unlikely*, Rhodes thought. *For one thing, if Finkelstein's only motive was to harm Emily, he could've easily hurt or killed her by now. He had ample opportunity. Why go through the charade with Mathias Lotta? There was nothing linking the two men. What about George Moll and Kyle Summers? What had they done to Finkelstein?*

Rhodes could find nothing that answered those questions.

He shook his head. This was not what it seemed. Someone wanted Mathias Lotta dead, and he or she had created this entire scheme to get to him. The only person with the motive to harm Mathias was his father, but Rhodes had no proof Ansel Lotta was behind this. He was not even sure if Lotta was capable of murder. However, that did not mean Lotta could not have hired someone to commit the crimes on his behalf.

It made sense when Rhodes thought about it. Lotta knew the FBI would not let him get close to Mathias. So he had someone murder Moll and Summers. He made it look like they were revenge killings for what they had done years before. He then kidnapped Emily and used her to incite a protest outside the hospital. He knew the public would want Mathias's head in return for the safety of a wife and mother.

*Was Finkelstein his accomplice?* Rhodes wondered. Maybe he was the one who had murdered Moll and Summers. He could have also been the one to kidnap Emily. When Finkelstein had outlived his usefulness, Lotta had killed him and made it look like a suicide.

Rhodes frowned. It sounded like he was fishing for answers. He was so desperate to pin the entire thing on Lotta that he was coming up with theories and conjecture.

Rhodes still needed to speak to Jo. He needed her to make sure Emily's case was not closed. Someone had driven the Fiat out of that street *after* Simon heard the gunshot. The FBI had to find out who it was.

Rhodes looked down the street. Jo's Jetta was not in the driveway.

*I should come back some other time.*

He peered through the window, looking in between the drapes, and saw nothing but darkness. There was no indication anyone was inside.

He pulled out a piece of paper and wrote, *Call me as soon as possible. Rhodes.*

He added the pay phone number to the paper, folded it, and began to wedge it in between the door and the wall.

He realized the door was unlocked.

He looked around. There was no one on the street.

He thought about not going in, but then decided he would wait for her inside. When he spoke to her, he would tell her to be careful and lock her doors.

He went in and immediately found himself staring at the walls of the living room. It looked like someone had recently removed something that was stuck to them. The paint was darker in certain areas, lighter in others.

He found pieces of paper inside the garbage bin that were torn, crumpled, or folded. He then caught something on one of the walls. They looked like newspaper clippings. The dates on them told him the clippings were decades old.

He looked around. All the other clippings had been trashed, but these were purposely left on the wall. *Odd*, he thought.

He then noticed something. He looked closer. Someone had underlined in red ink one name in particular on each of the clippings, adding a question mark afterward.

*Ansel Lotta?*

Rhodes had a feeling that Jo had found something, and he knew exactly where she had gone to confirm it.

## SEVENTY-TWO

Jo woke up and found she was unable to move. She felt groggy and it took a minute for her vision to clear. She was in a room. She was not sure how she got there.

She tried to think, but her head hurt. She closed her eyes to relieve the pain, but then she heard a voice.

"You are awake," Ansel Lotta said.

Jo remembered being in Lotta's house, and then she remembered darkness falling over her.

She lifted her head and saw Lotta standing in the corner. "Where am I?" she asked.

"In a place where no one can find you," he replied.

She looked around. The walls were bare, and there were no windows. She looked down. Her hands and ankles were shackled to a wooden table.

"I know who you are," she said.

He smiled. "Who am I?"

"You're the Bridgeton Ripper."

His smile widened. "It has taken you so long to finally put the pieces together. I was certain no one would."

"Your son did," she said.

Lotta's smile faded. "He found out. I wish he didn't, but he did." He walked to the other side of the room. He paused and then looked at her. "I guess, now that you are here, you want answers. I will oblige only because there is nowhere for you to go." He cleared his throat. "My father was a very wealthy man. He owned businesses across the country. But he also had a secret. He had this house built in the middle of nowhere for his mistress and his other children. You see, my father had a second family, one my mother never knew about. My father was always away, and we were told it was for his business. I believed him, and why wouldn't I? He was extremely successful. But as I grew up, I became suspicious he was hiding something. On a number of occasions, when he was angry at me, he would call me a different name. He would quickly correct himself, but I knew it was a name he had said so many times that it was on the tip of his tongue. One day when he was heading for one of his business trips, I snuck into the backseat of his car. I didn't realize it would take me to this place. He never knew I found out, but I vowed that once he was gone, I would take possession of this place. I did right after his death. I threw out his mistress and my step-siblings. The property was under my father's name, and as the sole beneficiary, I could do whatever I wanted. I then began to use the property for my experiments."

Jo's eyes widened. "You butchered your victims here."

"I prefer to call them medical examinations. As a surgeon, what better way to learn than to perform on live patients?"

Jo was speechless with horror.

Lotta said, "Like I had followed my father to this house, one day, Mathias did the same and followed me. What he saw forever changed his life. I had brought my last victim here…"

"Tara Millwood," Jo said.

He sighed. "It was eighteen years ago, and it was a mistake I regret even to this day. I should have stopped right after what happened to Mathias's mother, but I couldn't help myself. I needed the thrill of another kill."

"You killed Mathias's mother," Jo said. "You killed your own wife."

Pain contorted his face. "Mathias was only twelve when he found out my secret. It didn't take long for him to know I was the Bridgeton Ripper. This led him to question his mother's death. You may not know this, but it was my wife who alerted your father about me. She had seen me disappear on the nights of the murders, and soon she realized something was up. I know she loved me, but she also feared me. She feared our son would end up like me—a killer— or worse that I would kill her and our son. Ironically, I did end up killing her, and our son did end up becoming a killer. Anyway, I overheard her make the call to your father. He was always in the papers as the Bridgeton Ripper investigator, so he was well-known in the city. On that day, my wife thought I had left for school, but I had forgotten one of my assignments. When I returned to the house to pick it up, I caught her conversation with your father. It was then that I realized I had to make a decision. It was either her life or mine. I chose my survival over hers."

Jo stared at him.

"She told your father I disappeared between the hours of midnight and four a.m. She was right. It was at this time that I would procure myself a victim and take him or her to this very house and do my experiments. She obviously was not aware of this place, but she told him enough for him to follow me one night. I led him to this house. As he approached the front door, I snuck up from behind and subdued him, much like what I did to you."

Jo looked away. She could not believe she had let him get the drop on her.

Lotta said, "I had your father on the very table you are on now. And I enjoyed every minute of cutting him up."

Jo bit her bottom lip to control her emotions.

"Your father screamed and begged for me to stop, but I ripped every organ out of him. I made sure to give him enough drugs so that he was awake to see and physically feel it happening to him."

Jo broke down, crying.

## SEVENTY-THREE

Rhodes was at Ansel Lotta's house.

He rang the doorbell again and again, but there was no answer.

He was certain Jo came to see Lotta, but where was Lotta? His Bentley was still parked in the driveway.

He peered through the front door window and saw something on the floor of the hallway.

He scanned the neighborhood. The street was empty.

He smashed the front glass with his elbow and unlocked the door.

He entered. The house was eerily quiet. He moved further into the hallway.

As he got closer, the object on the floor materialized into a ceramic bowl. It had shattered into a dozen pieces. Its contents, mostly keys and spare change, were scattered all over the marble tiles.

Standing in the hallway, Rhodes rubbed his temples. He needed to think. A struggle must have occurred, and Lotta or Jo had left in a hurry.

*But where did they go?*

He shook his head. He had no proof that anything had happened. He was not sure if Jo had even come here. He had just broken into someone's house. If anyone found out, he would be back in jail.

He was debating what to do next when he noticed something underneath the entry table. He picked it up. It was Jo's cell phone.

His instincts were correct. She was here and something did happen. His foot hit a set of keys. He knelt down and picked them up. They belonged to the Bentley.

He rushed out and got inside the vehicle.

He turned it on and began flipping through the GPS.

He was not sure what he was looking for, but he was grasping for anything and everything.

The GPS had saved the last twenty addresses, and Rhodes realized that one address had come up several times.

*It's probably a wild goose chase*, he thought. *But I've got to do something.*

Rhodes set the location on the GPS and drove out of the driveway.

## SEVENTY-FOUR

"You're a monster," Jo said.

"I'm a man of science," Lotta replied. "In order to help many, you must at first hurt a few."

Jo stared at him. She had to keep him talking. There was still so much she wanted to know. All her adult life, she had been obsessed with the Bridgeton Ripper case, and now the Ripper was standing before her.

"Why did you choose to leave your victim's bodies under the bridges?" Jo asked.

"Look around you," Lotta replied. "We have the most bridges of any city in the country. Even the name of our city has the word 'bridge' in it. What most people don't realize is that bridges at night are dark and dangerous. A lot of activities can go unnoticed. People use them to jack up on drugs. People use them for a quick tryst. Even illegal transactions can be made underneath a bridge. During my residency, I had to go to various sites and provide medical services to the homeless and the drug addicts. You wouldn't believe how many dead bodies I came across under a bridge. It was then that I realized it was a perfect place to dump a body without arousing suspicion. I just never thought it would lead me to become the Bridgeton Ripper."

"Why did you do it? Why kill all those people?" Jo asked.

"Scientific curiosity, at first. I wanted to dissect a living, breathing human being. I wanted to see what was possible without any rules or restrictions."

"You tortured them."

"You may call it that. But I prefer *experimentation*. You wouldn't believe how many people have died in order for science to progress. Countless men, women, and children have endured unimaginable pain so others can have a better life. People have been used as guinea pigs throughout history. What I've done is nothing new."

Jo scowled. "You sound like that Nazi, Dr. Mengele."

Lotta scoffed. "I am no Nazi."

"But you enjoyed hurting your victims."

"Like I said, not at first, but then something changed. I would be lying if I told you I didn't begin to get some pleasure out of it."

"They were innocent people. They never harmed you."

"They weren't innocent."

Jo's eyes widened.

"One was a prostitute, another was a pimp, the third was a pedophile, and the fourth was a dirty lawyer who protected these kinds of people. They all deserved what they got."

"And what about your wife?" Jo asked. "What did she do to deserve it?"

"She betrayed me!" It was the first time Lotta had raised his voice. "That was her sin. Whatever happened to 'for better or worse,' or 'in sickness and in health?' She was my wife and my partner. She was supposed to protect me and not try to hurt me."

"And my father?" Jo asked. "He *was* innocent."

Lotta paused. "Well, he may have been more innocent than the others, but his sin was that he wanted to capture me, and back then, they would've given me the electric chair. In your father's case, self-preservation trumped everything else."

"What about Tara Millwood?" Jo asked. "What was her sin?"

Lotta sighed. "Again, she was a mistake. She hadn't done anything except that she was there that night alone, and I badly needed another kill."

Jo fidgeted against her restraints. "What are you going to do with me? Is my sin that I found out who you really are?"

He smiled. "As a matter of fact, it is. You see, when you graduated from the FBI academy, one of the local newspapers had an article on you. They asked why you had followed in your father's footsteps and became an agent, and your answer was that you wanted to capture the Bridgeton Ripper. Since then, I've been keeping an eye on you. I know you have been following up on all the leads to the case. Several times, I thought you had discovered something that would lead directly to me."

He paused a moment before he said, "On the night we drove to the water facility, I was certain you would find out the truth. I was aware that the two of you were in a relationship. I knew there was a reason he wanted you to bring me to him. Fortunately, I got to him before he could get to me."

"You shot your own son. What kind of father are you?"

He shrugged. "It's nature," he said. "Male lions will kill their own cubs if they feel they are a threat. I did what I did to survive."

He then moved to the other side of the room. He removed a black cloth that covered a metal trolley, revealing a tray filled with medical tools.

"I was hoping one day you would end up on my table," he said. "I wanted to make you feel what your father felt when he was on it."

## SEVENTY-FIVE

Rhodes had driven for an hour, and he still had no idea where he was going.

Wherever the GPS told him to turn, he did. He was following its instructions to the letter.

He was far from the city, with the nearest gas station over a mile away. There was nothing but trees, bushes, and grass on either side of him.

Suddenly, the GPS instructed him to get off the main road. He did and found himself driving on a dirt path.

He was not sure where he was going until he spotted a building up ahead.

The house must have been stylish and elegant at one time, but now it was ugly and dilapidated. Most of the roof shingles had come off, the exterior paint was chipped or peeled, and weeds and other wildflowers surrounded the house.

Rhodes parked the Bentley a good distance from the house. He was not sure why the GPS had brought him here, but he was not about to drive up unannounced.

He got out and carefully walked toward the house. When he was twenty feet away, he saw Jo's Jetta parked next to the home.

Rhodes moved toward the Jetta and peered inside. It was empty.

He pulled on the door and found it was unlocked. He found the keys still in the ignition. He quickly rummaged through the interior but found no weapon.

*Damn*, he thought. He did not want to go further without being prepared.

He popped the trunk and found a lug wrench in the back. He then approached the house.

He peered through the windows, but the interior was deserted. He then circled the house but found nothing that could hide two individuals.

*Where are they?* he thought. *I'm certain they're here.*

There was only one way to find out.

He went back to Jo's car. He grabbed the keys from inside and locked the doors. He then gripped the lug wrench and swung it against the side of the car.

The alarm came on.

Rhodes ran away and hid behind the Bentley.

## SEVENTY-SIX

Lotta pulled out a syringe. "I'm sure you already know what the other victims went through. I won't bother telling you what you are about to endure."

Jo knew full well what was coming. All the Ripper's victims were paralyzed while the good doctor performed his procedures on them. They may not have felt anything, but they could see and hear what was being done to them. The slicing of skin. The tearing of arteries. The sawing of bones. The ripping of organs. They lay helpless as their bodies were butchered before them.

Lotta came over. His lips were curled in an evil smile. "You will only feel a pinch."

He stuck the needle into her arm.

Jo could feel the cold liquid flow into her body.

"In less than half an hour, you will be completely paralyzed," he said.

He pulled the metal trolley closer and moved his fingers over the shiny instruments. His hand stopped at one and picked it up.

It was a scalpel.

"Why wait for the drug to take effect, I ask?" he said.

"I'll scream," she said, fear taking hold of her.

"Yes, you could, but may I remind you, we are in the middle of nowhere."

He tore open her shirt, exposing her abdomen. She was breathing heavily, and her stomach was moving up and down.

"We'll start from the navel and go all the way up," he said, relishing his every word.

He pressed the blade just below the belly button.

She closed her eyes. There was no point in calling for help. Even if she did, no one would come to save her.

She clenched her jaw. She would not beg or plead for her life. She would not give him the satisfaction. She would try to tolerate the pain as far as her body would let her. Sooner or later, she would succumb to his torture. She prayed she would be dead by then.

The blade began to cut into her skin when there was a noise.

She opened her eyes and saw that Lotta was standing still. His hands were frozen in position.

He listened for a moment, and then his shoulders relaxed. He went back to what he was about to do when the noise sounded again, and she realized it was coming from upstairs.

He put a finger to his lips and whispered, "You scream and I will cut your tongue out."

He quickly duct-taped her mouth and went up the stairs.

When he had shut the door behind him, Jo quickly looked around.

She had to find a way out.

Her head spun as she felt the drug taking effect.

She had to do something. But what?

The leather restraints held her arms firmly in place. There was no way for her to get out of them.

She spotted the scalpel. Lotta had dropped it on the trolley in a hurry. He did not realize that half the scalpel was over the edge.

It was just inches away from Jo's hand.

She twisted her wrists and stretched her fingers.

If she could somehow get to the blade, she could use it to cut her restraints.

She just hoped that whoever was upstairs could keep Lotta busy for a little while longer.

## SEVENTY-SEVEN

Rhodes watched as the front door slowly opened.

Out came Ansel Lotta. He was holding the same gun he had shot his son with.

Lotta looked around and then slowly moved toward the Jetta.

The alarm was wailing nonstop.

He tried opening the door, and when he realized the car was locked, he smashed the window with the butt of the gun and got behind the wheel.

After a few minutes of struggling, he was able to silence the alarm.

Lotta began to scan the area around the house.

Rhodes moved away from the Bentley, using the high grass and the bushes for cover. When he was a good distance away, he grabbed a stone and threw it at the Bentley.

It bounced off one of the tires.

He grabbed another one and threw it higher. This one landed squarely on the hood of the car.

The Bentley's alarm sounded.

Lotta began walking toward the car.

When the time was right, Rhodes dashed toward the house.

He raced up the steps and glanced back. Lotta was out of sight. He was probably halfway to the Bentley. The alarm was still blaring.

Rhodes entered the house. The smell of decay hung in the air.

The house was in terrible condition. There were holes in the floor, the walls had cracks, and the wallpaper was peeling. The carpet was stained, and in some places, curled up.

The house was spacious. Rhodes knew he had to hurry if he wanted to find Jo.

He checked the living room, the dining area, the hallway, even the office. He was making his way up the stairs when the Bentley's alarm went silent.

*Damn*, he thought. *He will be coming back.*

The floor creaked and cracked as he took each step up.

On the second floor, he paused and held his breath. The house was so old that even a slight movement could be heard throughout.

The front door swung open and Lotta came back in.

He moved past the stairs and disappeared into the hall.

Rhodes did not dare move. He just listened.

Lotta's footsteps echoed inside the house.

A door squeaked and then the footsteps faded.

Rhodes waited a good full minute before he carefully went downstairs.

He gripped the lug wrench and held it in front of him. In the hall, he spotted a door. A light gleamed underneath it.

Rhodes's steps were gentle and firm.

He reached for the door handle.

A loud noise sounded behind him.

Something hit him in the shoulder. He spun and looked behind him.

He saw Lotta standing in the hallway, gun aimed at him.

Rhodes grimaced as he placed a hand over the wound to control the pain. Before he could do anything, Lotta fired again, hitting Rhodes in the stomach.

He fell back. His head hit the floor with a loud thud.

He tried to move. Sharp pain coursed through his body.

Lotta stood over Rhodes, cocked his pistol, and aimed it at Rhodes's head. "Hello—and goodbye—Mr. Rhodes," he said.

## SEVENTY-EIGHT

Jo had managed to cut the leather restraint with the scalpel. With one hand loose, she was able to free herself from the table.

The drug was taking effect. She could not feel the tips of her fingers. Her legs were wobbly as she made her way to the stairs.

She heard footsteps from above.

She listened. The footsteps stopped at the door and then disappeared.

She heard another person's footsteps a minute later. These were heavy and measured.

She began to slowly make her way upstairs when she heard the gunshot, followed by another.

The next thing she heard was a loud thump. The floor above shook from the impact.

She did not wait to hear what happened next.

She clawed her way up the stairs, each step became more difficult than the one before. Her breathing was labored and she was sweating profusely.

She could feel herself losing control of her arms and legs. In a few minutes, she would be helpless.

She reached the top, grabbed the door handle, and with all her might, pushed it open.

She fell in the hallway and found herself lying in a pool of blood.

She looked up and saw a streak of crimson going through the hall and into the kitchen.

She followed the trail by crawling on her stomach.

# SAY YOUR PRAYERS

## SEVENTY-NINE

Rhodes was big and heavy, but even in his advanced age, Lotta was in great shape. "Actually, 'goodbye' not quite yet, Mr. Rhodes," he said, dragging Rhodes out into the backyard. "I have a better idea for your demise. Gunshots are so common a form of homicide, don't you think? Anyone can shoot another human being in cold blood."

Rhodes did not reply. His eyes were closed, and his breathing was labored, but he still lived.

"No," Lotta continued, "Your death will be special. You will die slowly, alive and fully aware of the pain I will put you through."

Lotta went around to a small shed and returned with a plastic container.

He unscrewed the cap. The smell of gasoline filled the air.

He began pouring the liquid over Rhodes.

"Let's see how a gallon of gasoline will affect the skin and organs of a living human," Lotta said as he emptied the last drops onto Rhodes.

He threw the container away, rummaged through his pockets, and pulled out a lighter.

"I wonder if you will scream," Lotta said, turning to walk a few steps back. "Since you are injured, perhaps—"

Something grabbed his leg.

Lotta looked down. Rhodes had circled his arms around his ankle and shin.

He tried to pull back, hoping Rhodes would lose his grip, but Rhodes held on for dear life.

He balled his fist and smashed it across Rhodes's head.

Rhodes held on.

He hit him again and again.

Rhodes still would not let go.

"My, Mr. Rhodes, you are a fighter," Lotta said between punches. "All that time living with criminals must have toughened you."

Rhodes yanked hard at Lotta's leg. He lost his footing and fell on his back.

Rhodes, summoning the last of his strength, yanked Lotta into the gasoline puddled on the lawn and then fell on top of him, coating Lotta's clothes with gasoline residue.

His large hands encircled Lotta's shirt collar.

Lotta desperately drew his gun and tried to aim it at Rhodes's head.

Rhodes's hand came out of nowhere and swatted the gun away, sending it flying toward the back steps.

Rhodes tightened his grip on Lotta's throat.

Lotta pulled his leg up and kneed Rhodes in the stomach, right next to the bullet wound.

Rhodes howled and fell off of him.

Lotta jumped up and then kicked him in the shoulder.

Rhodes thrashed as the pain shot through his entire body.

"I knew I should have killed you the moment I had the chance," Lotta screamed, his voice sounding slightly hoarse. "But now I'm going to enjoy seeing you suffer."

He moved away from Rhodes and held up the lighter.

He flicked it, but the flint failed to strike.

He flicked again and again.

On the fourth try, the lighter ignited.

"Goodbye, Mr. Rhodes," he said, the light flickering across his sinister smile. "I hope you burn in hell."

Rhodes did not bother to look up. He was in too much agony.

A gunshot rang in the air.

Lotta felt like a baseball bat had struck his chest.

He turned his face a mask of sudden pain and confusion.

Next to the house, near the back of the stairs, was Jo. She was on her stomach, looking directly at him. His gun was in her hands, and her eyes burned with pure hatred.

Lotta looked down. His shirt was covered in red.

He moved toward Jo and stumbled.

As he fell to his knees, clutching his chest, he could read the silent message in her eyes: *That was for my father*.

Lotta began to cough blood.

The lighter slipped out of his fingers.

"No!" he half screamed, half gurgled.

Rhodes rolled away as best he could.

# EIGHTY

Jo watched the lighter fall to the ground next to Lotta's shoes. The scene seemed to unfold in slow motion.

The flame touched the gas and ignited.

In a matter of seconds, flames engulfed Lotta.

He screamed and rolled on the ground, but it was futile. The fire raged on.

She watched as the Bridgeton Ripper cried for help.

"You… burn… in hell," she said, her lips barely moving.

Her entire body had gone numb.

The drug had taken full effect.

The screaming stopped. The smell of burnt flesh hung in the air.

She stared up at the sky, unable to do anything.

Her heart was no longer pounding. It was beating at a slower rate. The adrenaline was wearing off.

Her heart could only take so much. It had fought hard to get her to where she lay now at the back of the house. She knew her heart would not give up until she got the job done.

She also knew her time was up, and she accepted death with calm. Her father's killer was dead, and her mission in life was complete. She hoped that, wherever her father was now, he would be waiting for her with open arms and eyes full of love and pride.

She closed her eyes, awaiting her last breath.

# A FEW DAYS LATER

Jo opened her eyes and found Rhodes standing before her. He had a sling across one arm and a bandage on his face and forehead.

"Where… am… I?" she asked.

"You're in the hospital," he replied.

She tried to get up, but there were too many wires and tubes coming out of her body.

"What happened?"

"You had a heart transplant."

Jo was shocked. "How?"

"Apparently, you and Mathias had the same blood type, which made him a perfect donor."

Jo did not know what to say.

"You have Walters to thank for this. She had requested that the doctors preserve Mathias's heart after his death."

"What about Dr. Lotta?" Jo asked.

"He died in the fire."

"How did we get out of that house?" Jo said.

"I had your cell phone on me. I found it at Lotta's house. It didn't take long for your friends at the FBI to triangulate our location using your phone's GPS."

Jo touched her chest, right above where her heart was. "I can't believe it's done," she said, referring to the transplant. She had been avoiding it for so many years that she was certain it would never happen.

Rhodes said, "There was only a small window for the heart to be transplanted, and from what I've been told, you came close to not getting one."

"Didn't they need my consent?" she asked, curious.

"Your heart had failed, and the doctors took it upon themselves to do what they thought was necessary to save your life."

"I guess I don't have a choice now, do I?" she said.

Rhodes grinned. "You could tell them to take it out, you know."

"Did I just hear you tell a joke, Detective Rhodes?" Jo asked with a smile.

"I told you, I'm no longer a detective," Rhodes replied. "And I couldn't tell a joke even if someone shot me."

They both laughed.

Jo looked around the room. She saw several *Get Well Soon* balloons attached to her bed, as well as a few cards by her nightstand.

"Could you read those to me?" Jo asked Rhodes.

"Sure."

The cards were from Walters, Tarik, Irina, and Chris, as well as a joint one from Sam, Kim, and Chrissy.

"Thank you," she said after Rhodes finished the last card.

"You are welcome, and thank *you*," Rhodes replied.

Jo smiled. "Team effort."

"If you ever need any help, you know where to find me," Rhodes said.

Jo's smile widened as she thought of Chrissy's favorite form of promise.

"Pinky swear?" she asked.

Rhodes looked confused for a moment, but then he smiled.

.

Visit the author's website:
**www.finchambooks.com**

Contact:
**finchambooks@gmail.com**

Join my Facebook page:
**https://www.facebook.com/finchambooks/**

# MARTIN RHODES

1) Close Your Eyes
2) Cross Your Heart
3) Say Your Prayers
4) Fear Your Enemy

THOMAS FINCHAM holds a graduate degree in Economics. His travels throughout the world have given him an appreciation for other cultures and beliefs. He has lived in Africa, Asia, and North America. An avid reader of mysteries and thrillers, he decided to give writing a try. Several novels later, he can honestly say he has found his calling. He is married and lives in a hundred-year-old house. He is the author of the Lee Callaway Series, the Echo Rose Series, the Martin Rhodes Series, and the Hyder Ali Series.

Printed in Great Britain
by Amazon

38331571R00165